P9-CLE-973

# THE FIX
Volume One
*Where Beagles Dare*

*writer*
**nick spencer**
*artist*
**steve lieber**
*colors*
**ryan hill**
*letters/design*
**nic j shaw**

MARION COUNTY PUBLIC LIBRARY
321 MONROE STREET
FAIRMONT, WV 26554

JAN 1 3 2017

## Image Comics, Inc.

Robert Kirkman
Chief Operating Officer

Erik Larsen
Chief Financial Officer

Todd McFarlane
President

Marc Silvestri
Chief Executive Officer

Jim Valentino
Vice-President

Eric Stephenson
Publisher

Corey Murphy
Director of Sales

Jeff Boison
Director of Publishing Planning & Book Trade Sales

Jeremy Sullivan
Director of Digital Sales

Kat Salazar
Director of PR & Marketing

Branwyn Bigglestone
Controller

Sarah Mello
Accounts Manager

Drew Gill
Art Director

Jonathan Chan
Production Manager

Meredith Wallace
Print Manager

Briah Skelly
Publicist

Sasha Head
Sales & Marketing Production Designer

Randy Okamura
Digital Production Designer

David Brothers
Branding Manager

Olivia Ngai
Content Manager

Addison Duke
Production Artist

Vincent Kukua
Production Artist

Tricia Ramos
Production Artist

Jeff Stang
Direct Market Sales Representative

Emilio Bautista
Digital Sales Associate

Leanna Caunter
Accounting Assistant

Chloe Ramos-Peterson
Library Market Sales Representative

IMAGECOMICS.COM

## Indicia


THE FIX, VOL. 1: WHERE BEAGLES DARE. SEPTEMBER 2016. Regular Edition ISBN: 978-1-63215-912-0 Newbury Comics Variant Edition ISBN: 978-5343-0095-8 Big Bang Comics/Forbidden Planet Variant Edition ISBN: 978-1-5343-0096-5 Published by Image Comics, Inc. Office of publication: 2001 Center Street, 6th Floor, Berkeley, CA 94704.


Copyright © 2016 NICK SPENCER/STEVE LIEBER. All rights reserved. Originally published in single magazine form as THE FIX #1-4. THE FIX™ (including all prominent characters featured herein), its logo and all character likenesses are trademarks of NICK SPENCER/STEVE LIEBER, unless otherwise noted. Image Comics® and its logos are registered trademarks of Image Comics, Inc. No part of this publication may be reproduced or transmitted, in any form or by any means (except for short excerpts for review purposes) without the express written permission of Image Comics, Inc. All names, characters, events and locales in this publication are entirely fictional. Any resemblance to actual persons (living or dead), events or places, without satiric intent, is coincidental. PRINTED IN THE USA. For information regarding the CPSIA on this printed material call: 203-595-3636 and provide reference #RICH - 703342.

# THE FIX

## Volume One

### Where Beagles Dare

Image

FAMILY RESTAURAN

*I'M NOT GONNA LIE TO YOU...*

BEING A CRIMINAL THESE DAYS?
IT'S SHIT.

I MEAN, UNLESS YOU'RE THOSE RUSSIAN HACKERS THAT STOLE LIKE SIX BILLION WORTH OF CREDIT CARD NUMBERS FROM TARGET OR WHOEVER.

THOSE GUYS ARE DOING PRETTY GOOD.
BALMUSHKEV!

NO, BALMUSHKEV'S NOT A REAL WORD. THE FUCK DO I KNOW ABOUT RUSSIAN?
I DON'T THINK THEY WEAR THOSE HATS ANYMORE, EITHER.
SHAKE SHAKE

Bitcoin Wallet
File Settings Help
Overview
Send coins
Receive coins
Transactions
Address
Wallet
Balance: 8776.47 BTC
Unconfirmed: 40.00 BTC
Recent transactions
THESE INTERNET GUYS EVEN TOOK OVER DRUGS. "THE SILK ROAD" OR WHATEVER. SOUNDS DOWNRIGHT SCENIC.

WE ALL SAW IT COMING. WHO CARRIES CASH ANYMORE? NOT EVEN THE BANKS.
I'M SORRY, SIR, I CAN'T BREAK THAT.

EVEN HALF THE JEWELRY IS WORTHLESS NOW.
YOU KNOW YOU CAN'T USE THAT ON ANYBODY ELSE'S WRIST, RIGHT?
WATCH

YES SIR, TECHNOLOGY HAS CONSPIRED TO MAKE MOST OF YOUR RANK AND FILE HOODS AS OUTDATED AS THE CD PLAYERS WE USED TO RIP OUT OF CARS.

IT WAS EVOLVE OR DIE TIME, AND MOST OF THE BLACK MARKET WENT **VIRTUAL.**
PROSTITUTION, GAMBLING, IDENTITY FRAUD...WE THOUGHT WE WERE BIG TIME BACK IN THE DAY. TURNS OUT, WE WEREN'T EVEN SCRATCHING THE SURFACE.

ME, I KNOW AS MUCH ABOUT A FUCKING COMPUTER AS I DO RUSSIAN.
The Internet
FOR
ASSHOLES
Learn to:
• Add captions to cat photos
• Watch pornographic films without paying
• Harass women anonymously
Dr Mason Arboghast

I LIKE SOME KICKING...

THE OCCASIONAL BLUNT INSTRUMENT...
AND BEST OF ALL--

**A BIG GUN.**

MEN LIKE MYSELF--THE SMASH-AND-GRAB GUYS--WE'VE FOUND OUR OPTIONS DRAMATICALLY LIMITED, LEFT YEARNING FOR A SIMPLER, **BETTER** TIME--

THESE GUYS KNOW WHAT I'M TALKING ABOUT.
ALL RIGHT, OLD FUCKERS! NOBODY GETS CRAZY, NOBODY GETS HURT!
BINGO

PURSES AND WALLETS, WATCHES AND JEWELRY, ALL ON THE TABLE-- THAT'S IT, THAT'S IT-- THANK YOU VERY MUCH...

C...3...
THAT'S GREAT, KEEP IT COMING... NOW WHERE'S THE ORDERLY?
ALRIGHT, FINE, WHERE'S THE SUPERVISOR?
SHE'S ON BREAK.
HE'S OFF.
TAP TAP
OFF? WELL, WHO'S WATCHING YOU RIGHT NOW?

ARE YOU SERIOUS? JESUS CHRIST, THAT IS IRRESPONSIBLE--
HEY, HOLD ON--

SHE SAY C-3? THAT'S BINGO.

THAT'S FUCKING BINGO. SHOW SOME RESPECT.

WHAT ARE WE SUPPOSED TO DO?
I DUNNO, WATCH 'EM TIL SOMEBODY GETS BACK?
WHAT THE HELL IS GOING ON IN HERE?!!

THERE HE IS--
FINALLY. GUY JUST SHOWS UP WHEN HE FEELS LIKE IT--

PRETTY FUCKIN' INEXCUSABLE.
JESUS CHRIST--

TAKE US TO HIM.
AND I GET WHAT YOU'RE THINKING--

THIS IS PRETTY LOW, RIGHT?
LUNCH MENU
BUT I FIGURE THAT'S EXACTLY WHERE TO START--

JUST SO THERE'S NO CONFUSION. WE ARE NOT NICE GUYS--
WINK
SMILE

WE ARE NOT SYMPATHETIC PROTAGONISTS.
AND HEY, IF IT'S ANY CONSOLATION--

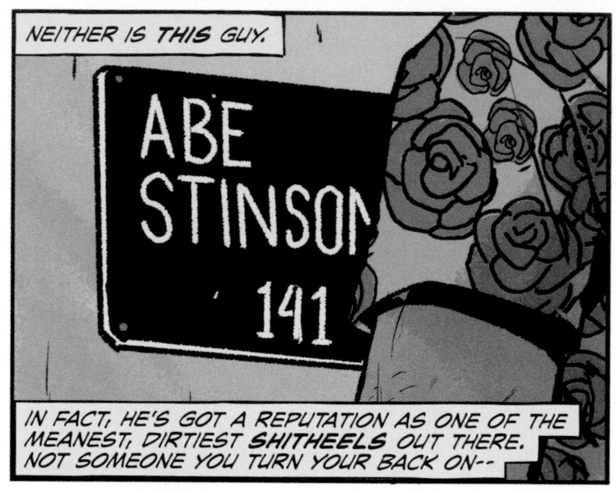
NEITHER IS THIS GUY.
ABE STINSON
141
IN FACT, HE'S GOT A REPUTATION AS ONE OF THE MEANEST, DIRTIEST SHITHEELS OUT THERE. NOT SOMEONE YOU TURN YOUR BACK ON--

THEN AGAIN, IT'S BEEN AWHILE.
FUCK-- IS THAT HIM?
S'AN OLD PHOTO. HE'S OUT, LET'S HURRY.

MAKES ME HAPPY I'M DEAD IN TEN YEARS TOPS, YOU KNOW?
I LOVE WHAT AN OPTIMIST YOU ARE. COME ON, HELP ME FIND IT. THE SMELL IN THIS PLACE IS FUCKING KILLING ME.

YEAH, WHAT IS THAT? IT'S LIKE WHEN YOU LEAVE MACARONI AND CHEESE OUT TOO LONG. AND DIRTY CARPET. HEY, HOLD ON--
YOU GOT SOMETHING?
YEAH...
YEAH...

IT'S HIS--
STASH!
FAP! FAP! FAP!

LOOK AT THIS! WOMEN NEXT TO POOLS. NO AIRBRUSH, NO DICK IN THE MOUTH... REAL SMILES! THIS IS CLASSIC SHIT.
WAIT A SEC--

RAK
CHK
FUCK!
FUCK!
AND SURE, NOW WE COME TO SOME OF THE LIMITATIONS INHERENT IN OUR MORE PHYSICAL APPROACH TO CRIME.

I MEAN, OF COURSE, THERE ARE RISKS.
BOOM

BUT REALLY-- WHAT DOESN'T?
RAK
CHK

FOR ME, IT'S A SMALL PRICE TO PAY TO NOT BE COOPED UP IN SOME CUBICLE, STARING AT A SCREEN ALL DAY--
EXIT

TRYING TO DEFRAUD MIDDLE MANAGEMENT TYPES BY PRETENDING TO BE A THIRTEEN-YEAR-OLD GIRL.

I MEAN, AT LEAST WITH MY APPROACH YOU GET SOME **EXERCISE**--

KEEPS YOU ON YOUR TOES.

YES SIR, A HEALTHY, ACTIVE LIFESTYLE IS GOOD FOR THE BODY **AND** MIND--

MAKES YOU FEELS LIKE YOU'RE MAKING THE **MOST** OF THINGS--
BOOM!

AND HELPS YOU APPRECIATE WHAT YOU HAVE.
I TAKE IT BACK, I WANNA LIVE *FOREVER.* YOU SEE HIM WITH THAT THING?
YEAH, IT KINDA ETCHED IN MY BRAIN WHEN I THOUGHT IT WAS GONNA TAKE MY HEAD OFF.
GUESS GETTIN' OLD'S NOT SO BAD.
MOSTLY TENS AND TWENTIES--THOUGHT THAT *NURSE* YOU WERE FUCKING SAID HE WAS RICH?

SHE'S IN COLLEGE--SHE DON'T EVEN KNOW WHAT *RICH* IS. AND I TOLD YOU, IT'S JUST FINGERS.
I APOLOGIZE, DIDN'T MEAN TO *BESMIRCH* HER HONOR.

YEAH, WELL, HOW MUCH WE LOOKING AT?
LOWER.

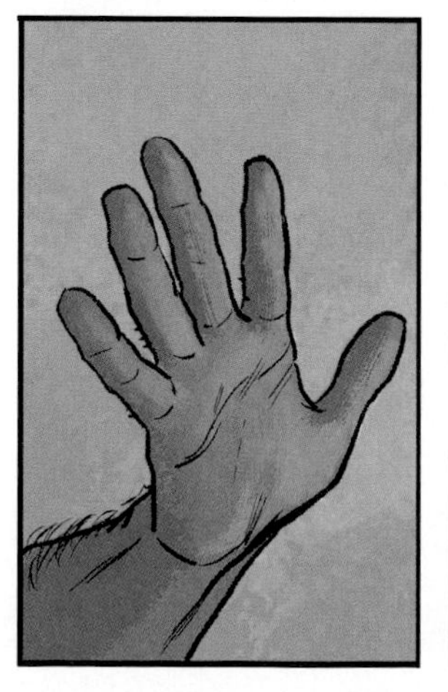

JESUS--WE *OWE* MORE THAN THAT.

MAYBE WE SHOULD SELL YOUR *POLAROIDS* THERE.

FUCK THAT, I'M KEEPING THESE.
I'M A RENAISSANCE MAN.
SO WHAT ARE YOU GONNA TELL JOSH?

I FIGURE I'LL TELL HIM YOU DIDN'T GRAB ENOUGH HOLDING ON TO YOUR BURIED TREASURE.
YOU MEAN MY NUTS?
HE'LL GIVE US MORE TIME. TRUST ME.

I DUNNO, MAN. YOU ALWAYS SAY THAT, AND THEN HE TELLS ANOTHER STORY ABOUT SOME GUY HE FED TO HIS SHARKS.
I THINK MAYBE HE'S TRYING TO SAY HE MIGHT FEED US TO HIS SHARKS. WHICH--
SHH, YOU HEAR THAT?
SKRRT!

LIKE I SAID BEFORE, BEING A CRIMINAL THESE DAYS IS SHIT--
ALL UNITS, ALL UNITS--129 WELLCHESTER, POSSIBLE ARMED ROBBERY--
DISPATCH, THIS IS 3-4-0-- YOU SAID 129 WELLCHESTER?
THAT'S RIGHT 3-40.
WE CAN TAKE THAT.
THAT'S WHY I GOT INTO LAW ENFORCEMENT.

THE

# FIX

I THINK IT WAS ALL THE TV WESTERNS THAT DID IT TO ME.
I WATCHED 'EM ALL WHEN I WAS A KID, AND NO MATTER WHAT--
I ALWAYS PULLED FOR THE BAD GUY.
I MEAN, IT DIDN'T MAKE ANY SENSE! I'M SUPPOSED TO ROOT FOR THIS ASSHOLE SHERIFF WHO ENDS UP SHOOTING SOME GUY FOR STEALING GOLD OR ROBBING A TRAIN?
OF COURSE YOU ROB A TRAIN! YOU LIVE IN A SHANTY! YOUR OTHER OPTIONS ARE DIE IN A MINE OR GET SYPHILIS FROM THE TOWN WHOREHOUSE.

BESIDES, THE BAD GUYS HAD THE COOLER OUTFITS. THEY HAD THE BETTER JOKES. THEIR HAIR WAS SHINIER.
I GUESS I JUST NEVER LIKED RULES.

WHERE THE OTHER KIDS WOULD HEAR "THIS IS FOR YOUR OWN GOOD" OR "YOU'LL UNDERSTAND WHEN YOU'RE OLDER," I KNEW IT WAS A CON.
TEACHER

YOU HAD TO BEHAVE AND GET GOOD GRADES SO YOU COULD GET INTO COLLEGE.

YOU NEEDED COLLEGE 'CAUSE YOU HAD TO GET A JOB.

YOU GOT THE JOB BECAUSE YOU NEEDED TO BUY A HOUSE, SO YOU COULD HAVE A FAMILY, WIFE AND KIDS.

AND IF YOU DID **ALL** THAT--WHEN YOU WALKED OUT YOUR FRONT DOOR TO GET THE MAIL, IN YOUR **CARDIGAN SWEATER** AND YOUR **KHAKIS**, YOUR NEIGHBORS WOULD ALL SMILE AT YOU AND NOD, AND THINK TO THEMSELVES--

AND THE HOUSE SURE AS SHIT AIN'T EITHER. DID WE MENTION **TAXES?** OR THAT THOSE KIDS ARE GONNA ASK YOU FOR **THEIR** COLLEGE MONEY SOMEDAY?

**OH,** AND YOUR **NEIGHBOR?** HE THINKS YOU'RE A FAT ASSHOLE, JUST LIKE HE IS. AND HE'S SLEEPING WITH YOUR **WIFE,** BY THE WAY, 'CAUSE THE GRASS IS ALWAYS GREENER ON THE OTHER FAT ASSHOLE.

BLAM
FDIC
TO MEET ONE IN THE FLESH.

ALL RIGHT, LET'S ALL BE *COOL*, YEAH?!
LADIES AND GENTLEMEN, YOU SEEM LIKE *INTELLIGENT* FOLKS--
SO YOU PROBABLY ALREADY GUESSED BY NOW-- THIS IS A *ROBBERY.*

NOW IF YOU COULD ALL *KINDLY* PLACE YOUR CASH, JEWELRY, AND OTHER ITEMS IN THE BAGS MY PARTNERS ARE BRINGING BY, WE CAN ALL BE ON OUR WAY *POST-HASTE*--
BABY
HEY...

YOU GOT SOMETHING TO SAY, *LITTLE MAN?*
YOU'RE NOT WEARING A *MASK.*
SKRITCH SKRITCH
WELL, NO, I AM NOT.
AND YOU KNOW *WHY* THAT IS?

IT'S SO YOUR *MOMMA* CAN SEE WHAT A *PRETTY* FACE I GOT.
I WAS IN AWE.

HE WAS THE *COOLEST, BADDEST* GUY I'D EVER SEEN--
NOW, ABOUT THAT *SAFE,* WHY DON'T WE--

UNTIL HE WASN'T.

*FUCK YEAH.*

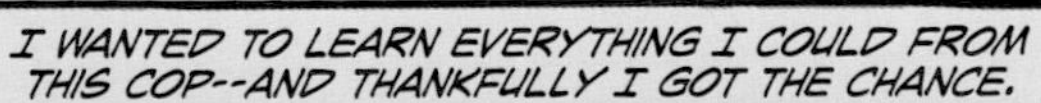

YES SIR, THE THREE WEEKS THAT GUY FUCKED MY MOM WERE THE **BEST** OF MY YOUNG LIFE.

AND AFTER THAT, I KNEW **EXACTLY** WHAT I WANTED TO BE--

JUST START AT THE *BEGINNING.*

I TOLD YOU--THEY JUST BUSTED IN HERE, DEMANDED I TAKE THEM TO *MISTER STINSON'S* ROOM. YOU SHOULD REALLY TALK TO HIM--
*WE WILL.*
SWISS MISS
MILK CHOCOLATE
FLAPPA FLAPPA FLAP
IN THE *MEANTIME*--CAN YOU TELL US WHAT THEY LOOKED LIKE?

THEY WERE WEARING *MASKS!*
LIKE, HALLOWEEN MASKS? LIKE THE *SCREAM* GUY?
NO, SKI MASKS.
*MM. CLASSIC.*

YEAH, BUT--DO YOU THINK YOU WOULD'VE BEEN MORE INTIMIDATED IF THEY'D BEEN WEARING MASKS LIKE THE SCREAM GUY? LIKE IT WOULD'VE MADE YOU MORE *COOPERATIVE?*
WHAT?
NEVER MIND THAT. HOW ABOUT HOW *TALL* THEY WERE?

I DUNNO--I DIDN'T REALLY GET THE BEST LOOK AT THEM--THE ONE WITH THE *GUN* IN MY BACK WAS A LITTLE TALLER THAN THE OTHER GUY--

LIKE, HOW TALL?
ABOUT MY *PARTNER'S* HEIGHT, OR TALLER?
*EHH--* PROBABLY ABOUT RIGHT.

*MM,* AND BUILD? AGAIN, COMPARED TO MY *PARTNER* HERE.
YEAH, BOUT THE SAME I GUESS, I DUNNO?

SURE, SURE. IT CAN BE DIFFICULT TO RECALL THESE THINGS, I UNDERSTAND--BUT WHAT ABOUT THEIR *CLOTHING?* THEIR SHIRTS MAYBE, ANY DISTINCTIVE COLORS, OR *PATTERNS--*
YOU KNOW, I THINK THAT'S MAYBE *ENOUGH* QUESTIONS FOR NOW, DOC HERE'S BEEN THROUGH A LOT--

I WAS ALREADY PULLING A DOUBLE...
HEAR THAT? MAN'S *TIRED.*
YOU'VE BEEN A *BIG* HELP, SIR.
APPRECIATE YOU DOING YOUR CIVIC DUTY!

HAHAHA

YOU'RE AN *ASSHOLE*, YOU KNOW THAT?
WHO WEARS A FLORAL PATTERN SHIRT WHEN THEY COMMIT AN ARMED ROBBERY?
AND THEN SHOWS UP AGAIN HALF AN HOUR LATER IN THE *SAME FUCKING SHIRT!*

YOU SEE THIS JACKET? HOW IT'S NOT THE SAME ONE? 'CAUSE I GOT A *KEEN EYE* FOR THE LITTLE THINGS, MY FRIEND.
TUG
WELL, IT'S USED TO LOOKING AT YOUR COCK SO I'D IMAGINE THAT'S TRUE.

WAIT-- YOU HEAR THAT?
WHAT?
IT'S THE SOUND OF A *CAMERA BAG* BEING UNZIPPED.
TSST!
WE'RE LIKE NINETY FEET FROM THE DOOR! AT LEAST--
*AND YET.* WHY, YOU WANT THIS ONE?

MAN, YOU KNOW I HATE THAT BULLSHIT.
SUIT YOURSELF, BUT MY OPINION?
YOU'RE MISSING THE *WHOLE POINT.*

BECAUSE, YES, BEING ABLE TO PARK WHEREVER YOU WANT IS GREAT.
HONK HONK
♫

AND GATHERING EVIDENCE SURE CAN BE...
EVIDENCE
NCE

A PRETTY GOOD TIME.
BUT FOR MY MONEY--OR THE OLD GUY'S MONEY WE JUST STOLE, I GUESS--
EVIDENCE

THIS IS THE BEST PART OF THE JOB.
ANYONE WHO WOULD TERRORIZE OUR SENIORS LIKE THIS REPRESENTS THE ABSOLUTE WORST SOCIETY HAS TO OFFER--
IT'S CRIMES LIKE THIS THAT SHAKE MY FAITH IN HUMANITY TO ITS VERY CORE.

DETECTIVE--WHAT ABOUT THE VICTIM IN THIS CASE? HAVE YOU BEEN ABLE TO TALK TO HIM YET?
HIS DOCTOR HAS ADVISED THAT WE LET MISTER STINSON REST FOR NOW--HE'S OBVIOUSLY BEEN THROUGH A TRAUMA--BUT WE'RE EAGER TO SPEAK WITH HIM, OBVIOUSLY.

AND I WOULD JUST LIKE TO TAKE A MOMENT--
TO URGE ANYONE WHO HAS INFORMATION ABOUT THIS CRIME,
TO COME FORWARD AND ASSIST US WITH OUR INVESTIGATION AND TO DO SO IMMEDIATELY.
BECAUSE, REST ASSURED, WE WON'T STOP UNTIL WE'VE CAUGHT WHOEVER IS RESPONSIBLE FOR THIS. THIS TIME--

I'M TAKING IT PERSONALLY.
NOW YOU'RE PROBABLY THINKING, "THAT'S IT? THAT'S WHAT HE'S IN IT FOR? A CHEAP HEADLINE?"
BUT THING IS, IN THE RIGHT HANDS--

IT'S NOT CHEAP AT ALL.
THERE HE IS! MY BIG FUCKING HERO! KEEPING THE STREETS SAFE!
YOU SEE THE NEWS?

YEAH--I CAN'T BELIEVE THAT SHIT. HOW'S A FOUR-YEAR-OLD DRIVE A CAR? I MEAN, HOW'S HE EVEN REACH THE PEDALS? FUN AS HELL WATCHING THE COPS CHASE HIS ASS, THOUGH.
NO, BEFORE THAT--THE RETIREMENT HOME THING!

OH, RIGHT. YOU WERE ON, WEREN'T YOU?
SORRY ROY, I WAS KINDA CHECKING MY PHONE THROUGH IT. FUCKING TINDER. LET ME ASK YOU SOMETHING, THOUGH--
YOU EVER TASTED YOUR OWN CUM?
SORRY?

YOU KNOW, LIKE, WHEN YOU WERE A KID, 'CAUSE YOU WERE CURIOUS?
I DON'T REALLY HAVE AN INQUISITIVE NATURE.
RIGHT, BUT WHAT ABOUT ACCIDEN-TALLY?
LIKE, YOU DID A HANDOFF AND YOU THOUGHT YOU CLEANED IT UP,
BUT THEN YOU SNEEZED AND YOU'RE LIKE, OH SHIT, I FORGOT.
GUESS I'VE BEEN LUCKY SO FAR.

YEAH, ME TOO--BUT THE OTHER NIGHT, I'M FUCKING, RIGHT?
A WOMAN. AND SHE'S GOT ME IN THIS--WELL, IT'S A WEIRD POSITION...
KINDA UPSIDE DOWN...
LIKE MY ANKLES ARE UP BY MY HEAD, AND MY HEAD'S ON THE FLOOR, AND MY ASS IS ON THE SOFA...
AND HER TONGUE IS UP THERE--

--AND AT FIRST I'M THINKING THIS IS FUCKING GREAT!
BUT THEN I START GETTING CLOSE, RIGHT?
AND IT'S JUST STARING DOWN AT ME.
COBRA COMMANDER.
YOU'VE SEEN IT RIGHT? COBRA-LA?
THEN YOU KNOW WHAT I MEAN.
HE'S WORTHY OF FEAR AND RESPECT.
I GOT THE DICK YOU GET WHEN STANLEY TUCCI PUTS YOU IN A METAL CHAMBER SO YOU GOT ONE BIG ENOUGH TO FUCK NAZIS.
AND HE'S READY.
BUT SHE'S GOT THE LEVERAGE AND SHE'S SO SLAMMED ON ECSTASY--
SO I'M LIKE, HEY, YOU GOTTA LET ME UP, BITCH!
PLUS WITH GRAVITY, I GUESS IT ALL HAPPENS FASTER.
ANYWAY, POINT IS--I TOOK THE HIT, RIGHT?

*SO, THIS IS **DONOVAN.** AND BELIEVE IT OR NOT--*

THIS IS HIM ON A GOOD DAY.
ALL UNITS, ALL UNITS--
EMERGENCY ASSISTANCE REQUIRED AT THE GROVE. MULTIPLE CALLS REPORTING--
WHAT THE FUCK?

ES&NOBLE
KSELLERS
The Internet
ASSHOLES

NEW YORK

WELL, MISTER DONOVAN, WE'VE GOT A LOT OF CHARGES TO GO OVER, SO LET'S BEGIN WITH--
GONNA STOP YOU RIGHT THERE, OFFICERS--

I WOULD JUST LIKE TO SAY-- IN MY DEFENSE, THAT WAS MY FIRST TIME DOING BATH SALTS, AND I CAN ASSURE YOU, NEXT TIME, I WILL BE MUCH BETTER PREPARED.
THE NEXT TIME?
YEAH, LIKE I WAS THINKING--
MY DOMINATRIX, SHE'S GOT THIS HARNESS THING SHE USES, SAYING I FLINCH LIKE A LITTLE BITCH AT THE CANDLE WAX--IT'S ACTUALLY VERY DEMEANING--

BUT ANYHOW, I FIGURE NEXT TIME, I'LL GET HER TO COME OVER, STRAP ME IN BEFORE I DO IT. IT'S THE RESPONSIBLE THING TO DO--
BECAUSE I NOW KNOW THE POWER OF THIS TERRIBLE, TERRIBLE DRUG.
POP
POP
POP

YEAH, WELL, JAMBA JUICE KNOWS IT, TOO--YOUR CAR'S STILL STUCK IN THEIR KIOSK. PUT ONE OF THEIR EMPLOYEES IN THE HOSPITAL.
THAT'S AWFUL. I'LL BE SURE TO MAKE A SIZEABLE DONATION TO MISTER JAMBA'S RECOVERY.
YOU TRIED TO TAKE A MIME'S FACE OFF.
HIS ACTUAL FACE, OR HIS MIME FACE?

MISTER DONOVAN, I'M NOT IN THE HABIT OF RECOMMENDING THIS, BUT--ARE YOU SURE YOU DON'T WANT A LAWYER PRESENT?

AND CUT HIM IN ON FIVE PERCENT OF THIS? FUCK THAT.
HOW DO YOU THINK GETTING ARRESTED WORKS, EXACTLY?

I'M A LITTLE CONFUSED MYSELF. I'M LOOKING AT YOUR RECORD HERE, AND IT'S--PRETTY SUBSTANTIAL. BUT MOST OF THE TIME I SEE CHARGES DROPPED, WARNINGS ISSUED--HOW EXACTLY--
AW, THAT'S EASY--
YOU GUYS LIKE MOVIES?
SORRY?

I'M A PRODUCER.

I HAVE A FIRST LOOK DEAL AT UNICORN PICTURES. YOU KNOW WHAT THAT MEANS?

IT MEANS I GET SHIT MADE, YOU KNOW?

YOU'VE SEEN MY STUFF--ALIENZ? THE PREQUEL TO RESURRECTION? DID THAT. THAT COCOON PORN PARODY? DID THAT.
THING IS, A LOT OF WHAT I MAKE IS ABOUT YOU--COP STORIES.
LIKE RIGHT NOW, I GOT THIS THING, JAKE GYLLENHAAL AND DENZEL, AND THEY'RE BEAT COPS, BUT ONE OF 'EM'S CROOKED AS SHIT.
...YOU MEAN LIKE TRAINING DAY?
HUH? WHAT? NO--
THAT WAS ETHAN HAWKE.

RIGHT, BUT THEY WERE BEAT COPS, AND DENZEL WAS CROOKED-- KINDA SOUNDS THE SAME.
WHY WOULD YOU ASSUME DENZEL'S CROOKED?
YOU A FUCKING RACIST?
WHOA, HEY--

I'M KIDDING, I'M KIDDING. JAKE'S THE BAD GUY THIS TIME--AND GET THIS, HE'S GAY.
YOU MEAN LIKE IN BROKEBACK MOUNTAIN?

BROKEBACK--DUDE, I TOLD YOU, THIS IS A COP MOVIE!
LOOK, POINT IS--YOU KNOW WHAT THE BEST THING I CAN FLASH IN FRONT OF ONE OF MY MOVIES IS?

"INSPIRED BY TRUE EVENTS." GIVES US INSTANT CRED WITH THE AUDIENCE.
AND THING IS, TO MAKE A MOVIE OUT OF THE STUFF YOU'VE REALLY DONE--
WE'D HAVE TO BUY THE RIGHTS TO THAT STORY.
WE CALL IT AN OPTION.

I SEE... AND ONE OF THESE OPTIONS--HOW MUCH WOULD YOU SAY WE'D GET?

FOR THE OPTION ITSELF, FORTY GRAND? MAYBE MORE?
BUT HERE'S THE THING, FELLAS-- IF WE MAKE THAT MOVIE--
IF IT GETS THE GREEN-LIGHT--

THIS IS WHAT YOU'RE LOOKING AT.

SO WE LET HIM OFF WITH A WARNING. I MEAN, KIDS, RIGHT?
HAHAHAW

AND NOT TOO LONG AFTER THAT, WE SIGNED AN OPTION DEAL FOR "FINAL MARKDOWN"--THE STORY OF OUR HARROWING ADVENTURE TAKING ON A DRUG-ADDLED MADMAN IN A SHOPPING CENTER.
IT'S DIE HARD... IN A FUCKING MALL.
OOH, I LIKE THAT.
I LIKE MOVIES!

AND WE THOUGHT WE WERE RICH. EVERYONE SEEMED SO EXCITED, EVERYTHING WAS MOVING SO FAST.
THE CHECK CAME, AND WE THOUGHT, WHAT THE HELL? WE COULD LIVE DANGEROUSLY SEEING AS OUR LITTLE MOVIE WAS DEFINITELY GETTING MADE. THIS CASH WAS JUST THE START. WHY NOT TRY FOR DOUBLE OR NOTHING?
SO WE TOOK IT WHERE YOU ALWAYS TAKE YOUR MONEY WHEN YOU'RE LOOKING TO WIN BIG--

ILLEGAL BATTLEBOT BETTING RINGS.
C'MON VOMROCKET, C'MON--
DOOOO IT!!! DOOO IT!!!

BUT TURNS OUT, LUCK WAS NOT ON OUR SIDE.
WHAM!
AND THE WINNER IS--JIZZMOTRON!
LOOKING BACK, WE SHOULD'VE TAKEN IT AS A SIGN.

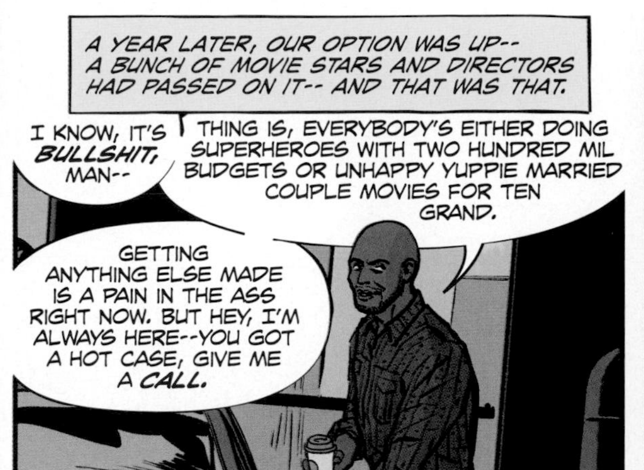
A YEAR LATER, OUR OPTION WAS UP-- A BUNCH OF MOVIE STARS AND DIRECTORS HAD PASSED ON IT-- AND THAT WAS THAT.
I KNOW, IT'S BULLSHIT, MAN--
THING IS, EVERYBODY'S EITHER DOING SUPERHEROES WITH TWO HUNDRED MIL BUDGETS OR UNHAPPY YUPPIE MARRIED COUPLE MOVIES FOR TEN GRAND.
GETTING ANYTHING ELSE MADE IS A PAIN IN THE ASS RIGHT NOW. BUT HEY, I'M ALWAYS HERE--YOU GOT A HOT CASE, GIVE ME A CALL.

WHICH IS WHAT PUTS ME HERE--
I MEAN, THE MOST VULNERABLE AMONG US!

I DUNNO, MAN--OLD PEOPLE?
NOBODY WANTS TO WATCH OLD PEOPLE FUCKING.

WHY WOULD THEY BE FUCKING?
SORRY, I WAS THINKING ABOUT SOMETHING ELSE. I REALLY TOOK A BATH ON THAT COCOON THING...
AND I WISH WE COULD CHALK THIS UP TO BEING A LEARNING EXPERIENCE--

WHAM!
BUT THAT WOULD REQUIRE LEARNING SOMETHING.

GODDAMN JIZZMOTRON, MAN.
HOW MANY TIMES?
NO SHIT. WHAT ARE WE GONNA TELL JOSH?
OKAY, WE SHOULD MAYBE START TO WORRY NOW.
WELL, YOU KNOW WHAT THE BEST POLICY IS SUPPOSED TO BE--

HOW'S THAT SAYING GO AGAIN?

WELL, LOOKIT THIS, ROY--IT'S OUR FAVORITE INTERNAL AFFAIRS OFFICER.
SHE'S NOT MY FAVORITE. I LIKE THAT GUY THAT WATCHES BONES. WE BONDED OVER THAT SHIT.
EITHER WAY, GOOD TO SEE YOU, LIEUTENANT MALONE.

BOYS, I TOLD YOU, YOU CAN CALL ME SHERYL.
JUST BECAUSE I'M IN I.A. DOESN'T MEAN WE NEED TO HAVE AN ADVERSARIAL RELATIONSHIP.
A LITTLE CLICHE FOR MY TASTES--
FOR INSTANCE, WHEN I WENT LOOKING FOR YOU, I KNEW TO SHOW UP HERE, AT AN ILLEGAL BETTING ESTABLISHMENT--
BUT YOU DON'T SEE ME WRITING ANY REPORTS, DO YOU?
NOW, THIS, ON THE OTHER HAND--

YOU FELLAS KNOW ANYTHING ABOUT THIS? ARMED ROBBERY AT A SENIOR CENTER THIS AFTER-NOON?
MIGHT BE WORTH MY TIME.

WELL, YEAH, OF COURSE WE DO, LIEUTENANT. WE'RE THE INVESTIGATING OFFICERS!
HM, RIGHT, I SAW THAT. WELL MAYBE THIS WILL HELP WITH YOUR INVESTIGATION--I MEAN IS THAT YOU TWO? IN YOUR CAR, ROY?
HM--LEMME SEE...
YEAH, LET'S TAKE A LOOK--
NO, NO, SEE--HERE WE GO--THIS CAR HAS ARIZONA PLATES. MY CAR HAS CALIFORNIA PLATES.
THAT'S RIGHT! PLUS, THESE GUYS ARE WEARING MASKS. WE'RE NOT WEARING MASKS.
YOU GOTTA BE KIDDING ME.
NOW, DON'T BEAT YOURSELF UP, LIEUTENANT, WE'RE DETECTIVES--WE'RE TRAINED TO SPOT THIS KIND OF THING.
WHAT YOU ARE IS A COUPLE OF SLOPPY ASSHOLES. YOU'RE ROBBING INVALIDS NOW?

HEY, YOU DIDN'T EVEN ASK IF WE GOT AN ALIBI--
THAT'S RIGHT. YOU SHOULD TALK TO JIZZMOTRON OVER THERE, HE'LL VOUCH FOR US.
FLAPPITY FLAP FLAP
YOU KNOW WHAT, IT DOESN'T EVEN MATTER, YOU TWO HAVE BIGGER THINGS TO WORRY ABOUT--

BECAUSE WHEN YOU'RE AT THE TOP OF THE ORGANIZED CRIME FOOD CHAIN, THESE ARE THE FIRST COPS YOU BUY--
THE BOSS WOULD LIKE TO SEE YOU.
INTERNAL AFFAIRS.

AND JOSH IS MOST DEFINITELY THE APEX PREDATOR IN THESE PARTS.
SO CAN I GET YOU GUYS A KOMBUCHA? COCONUT WATER?
YOU AT LEAST HAVE TO TRY SOME OF THESE KALE CHIPS. DID THEM MYSELF. A LITTLE OLIVE OIL, SOME PAPRIKA, HIMALAYAN SEA SALT. I'M PRETTY PROUD OF THEM.
ABSOLUTELY. THANK YOU, JOSH.
YEAH, THANKS, BOSS. CRUNCH
HEY WAIT, YOU GUYS DON'T HAVE GLUTEN ALLERGIES DO YOU?
UHH...
AH, I'M MESSING WITH YOU. OF COURSE THEY DON'T HAVE ANY GLUTEN. WHAT KIND OF A HUMAN BEING DO YOU THINK I AM?
ANYHOO, FIRST OFF, I REALLY APPRECIATE YOU GUYS COMING ALL THE WAY OUT TO VENICE, I KNOW THE TRAFFIC'S A NIGHTMARE.
I WOULD'VE COME OUT YOUR WAY BUT--
EVER SINCE THIS LITTLE GUY HAPPENED...
HEY, THAT REMINDS ME--YOU'VE SEEN THE HOME BIRTH VIDEO, RIGHT? WE SENT YOU THE DROPBOX LINK?
UM, YEAH-YEAH, WE GOT IT.
WATCHED IT A BUNCH OF TIMES.
PRETTY MAGICAL, RIGHT? BUT NOW MEGHAN'S BACK AT PWC, NOT TO MENTION HER LAUGHING YOGA AND THE HERB GARDEN--SO, BOTTOM LINE, I'M ON FULL-TIME DADDY DUTY THESE DAYS.
IT'S NOT ALL BAD, THOUGH. I AM BURNING THROUGH THIS AMERICAN LIFE EPISODES LIKE A HOUSE ON FIRE. BUT WE SHOULD GET DOWN TO IT, YEAH?
ARE WE GOING TO HAVE TO CARVE YOUR TAINTS OUT?
SO YEAH--

MEET JOSH.
OOH YOOO-SHHIII-MIII...

SO THE FARM IS ENTIRELY PESTICIDE FREE?

MUMPS IS A MYTH! OUR CHILD, OUR CHOICE!
JUST SAY "NO" TO MANDATORY VACCINATIONS
I DON'T WANT ANY

I'M SORRY, THAT--THAT GOT A LITTLE DARK.
OBVIOUSLY, THOUGH, YOU GUYS SEE THE TROUBLE I'M IN.
YOU'VE OWED ME MONEY FOR A VERY LONG TIME NOW.

NOT ONLY THAT, BUT NOW YOU'RE PULLING JOBS WITHOUT TALKING TO ME, WHICH GOES DIRECTLY AGAINST YOUR NON-COMPETE AGREEMENT--
I DUNNO, GUYS--I'M FEELING PRETTY UNDERVALUED HERE. AND I'M STARTING TO WORRY YOU DON'T HAVE ANY CONCRETE PLAN TO PAY ME BACK.
WELL, JOSH--SEE--WE HAVE ANOTHER STUDIO MEETING NEXT WEEK--

AND I BELIEVE IN YOU. YOU KNOW I'M NOT HERE TO DIMINISH YOUR DREAMS. BUT IN THE MEANTIME, I'VE GOT TO SEE SOME RETURN ON MY INVESTMENT--
THERE WERE ALL THOSE MURDERS WE COVERED UP FOR YOU.

AH, I DON'T THINK MAC MEANT--
NO, IT'S COOL. DOESN'T MATTER. THE THING IS, NEXT WEEKEND, MEGHAN AND I ARE SUPPOSED TO GO UP TO NAPA FOR THIS RETREAT--SOME REAL US TIME.

AND I JUST--IF I GO UP THERE WITH THIS HANGING OVER ME, I WON'T REALLY COMMIT. I JUST KNOW IT.
SO, I FIGURE WE GO AHEAD AND CARVE YOUR TAINTS OUT NOW, RIGHT? IT'S EASIER.

FUCK!
NO, NO, JOSH, COME ON NOW--

I'M SURE THERE MUST BE SOMETHING WE CAN DO. AND YOU'RE RIGHT--WE NEVER SHOULD'VE DONE THAT JOB WITHOUT RUNNING IT BY YOU FIRST.
JUST KNOW IT CAME FROM OUR ENTHUSIASM FOR GETTING THIS DEBT SETTLED.
YEAH, WE LOVE OUR TAINTS!

SIGH-- OKAY, OKAY. I DO HAVE ONE THING, ACTUALLY-- I DON'T KNOW THAT IT'S IN YOUR *WHEELHOUSE,* THOUGH...
YOU MEAN IT'S NOT A MURDER?

JUST TELL US WHAT IT IS, WE'LL MAKE IT HAPPEN.
WELL, IT'S FAIRLY STRAIGHT-FORWARD, ACTUALLY--
I JUST NEED YOU TO GET SOMETHING THROUGH *LAX* FOR ME.

AND AS SOON AS HE SAYS IT, WE ALREADY KNOW--

HE MIGHT AS WELL GO AHEAD AND DO THE WHOLE *CARVE-OUT* THING--

BECAUSE WE'RE ALREADY DEAD.

IT USED TO BE SO EASY, GETTING SHIT THROUGH CUSTOMS. GREASE THE RIGHT PALMS, CUT THEM IN ON THE ACTION--

BUT THAT WAS BEFORE HE SHOWED UP
OVER SIX HUNDRED ARRESTS JUST LAST YEAR, RESULTING IN THE SEIZURE OF TWO TONS WORTH OF ILLEGAL CONTRABAND.

HE IS THE MOST FEARED OFFICER IN THE ENTIRE LOS ANGELES POLICE FORCE. UNBEATABLE, UNSWERVING, AND INCORRUPTIBLE.

THEY CALL HIM PRETZELS.

PRETZELS THE DOG.

I GET WHAT YOU'RE SAYING--
WHERE'S THE DOG?
I WAS PROMISED A DOG.
BUT SEE; THERE'S A PROCESS TO THESE THINGS.
AND REMEMBER, LIKE THEY SAY, TO THOSE WHO WAIT--

IG THUNDER
50 FT.
PIRAL
1/4 MI.
UTTE


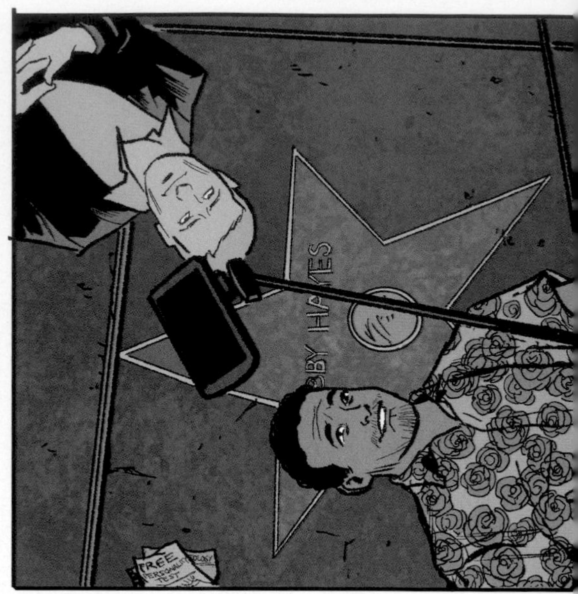

BBY HAYES
FREE PERSONALITY TEST

HOLLYWOOD

IN-N-OUT

JOB CITY

JAYNE MANSFIELD
1938 — 1967
WE LIVE TO LOVE YOU MORE EACH DAY
SNIFF

YOU HAVE A ***GREAT DAY,*** BUDDY?!

*AW,* YEAH, PARTNER! THE ***GREATEST!***

***GREAT!*** I'M GONNA ***SHOOT*** YOU NOW!

OKAY, OBVIOUSLY WE CAN'T SHOOT YOU IN THE ASS, BECAUSE OF THAT SOPRANOS EPISODE.
BUT I DID HAVE AN IDEA.

MY HAND?
IT'S A 9 MILLIMETER--YOU'RE NOT GONNA LOSE IT.
YOU DON'T KNOW THAT!

IT'S FAST AND EASY, THE BULLET WILL GO STRAIGHT THROUGH.
NO FUCKING WAY!
YOU WON'T. I LOOKED IT UP--
I DIDN'T LOOK IT UP.

APPARENTLY THE HUMAN HAND HEALS FASTER THAN ANY OTHER PART OF THE BODY.
BUT MAN, MY HAND--I USE IT. I USE IT...A LOT?
SURE, BUT THAT'S YOUR RIGHT. WE'LL SHOOT YOU IN YOUR LEFT.
I USE BOTH!

OH, CHRIST...
WHAT? YOU'RE IN A RELATIONSHIP WITH SOMETHING YOUR WHOLE LIFE, YOU GOTTA MIX IT UP!

LOOK, JUST PUT YOUR HAND UP LIKE YOU'RE GIVING ME A HIGH FIVE.
OR, YOU KNOW, A PRAISE JESUS, HALLELUJAH.
WHATEVER GETS YOU THROUGH IT.
EXPLAIN TO ME WHY WE'RE DOING THIS AGAIN?!
SO THAT JOSH DOESN'T TORTURE-MURDER US?
REMEMBER, MAC, HE MIGHT LET YOU KEEP THE HAND...
...BUT HE WON'T LET YOU KEEP WHAT YOU NEED IT FOR.

BUT WHY CAN'T YOU DO IT?
BECAUSE I'M ALLERGIC.
TO GETTING SHOT?
TO DOGS.

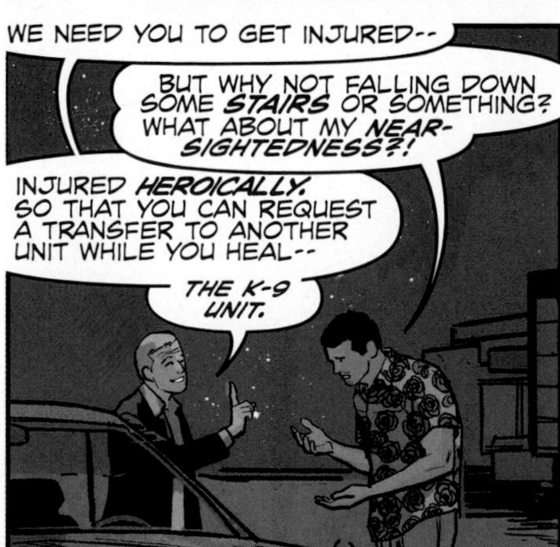
WE NEED YOU TO GET INJURED--
BUT WHY NOT FALLING DOWN SOME STAIRS OR SOMETHING? WHAT ABOUT MY NEAR-SIGHTEDNESS?!
INJURED HEROICALLY. SO THAT YOU CAN REQUEST A TRANSFER TO ANOTHER UNIT WHILE YOU HEAL--
THE K-9 UNIT.

I...I DO LOVE DOGS...

OF COURSE YOU DO.
YOU THINK I DON'T CHECK YOUR INSTAGRAM?
THIS IS GONNA BE GREAT, BUDDY--

MORE THAN WORTH A TEENSY WEENSY LITTLE BULLET HOLE.

OKAY, OKAY... JUST--MAKE IT QUICK.

GUNSHOTS USUALLY ARE.

AH, HELL--I DON'T KNOW IF I CAN DO THIS AFTER ALL.

SIGH
--OH, THANK CHRIST, MAN...
I DIDN'T WANT TO--

BLAM

NO, NO, I GOT IT.

DISPATCH, SHOTS FIRED, WE HAVE AN OFFICER DOWN!
I REPEAT, AN OFFICER DOWN--
FUCK! FUCK! FUCK! FUCK! FUCK! FUCK! FUCK! FUCK! FUCK! FUCK! FUCK! FUCK! FUCK! FUCK! FUCK! FUCK! FUCK!

FUCK
HEROICALLY.

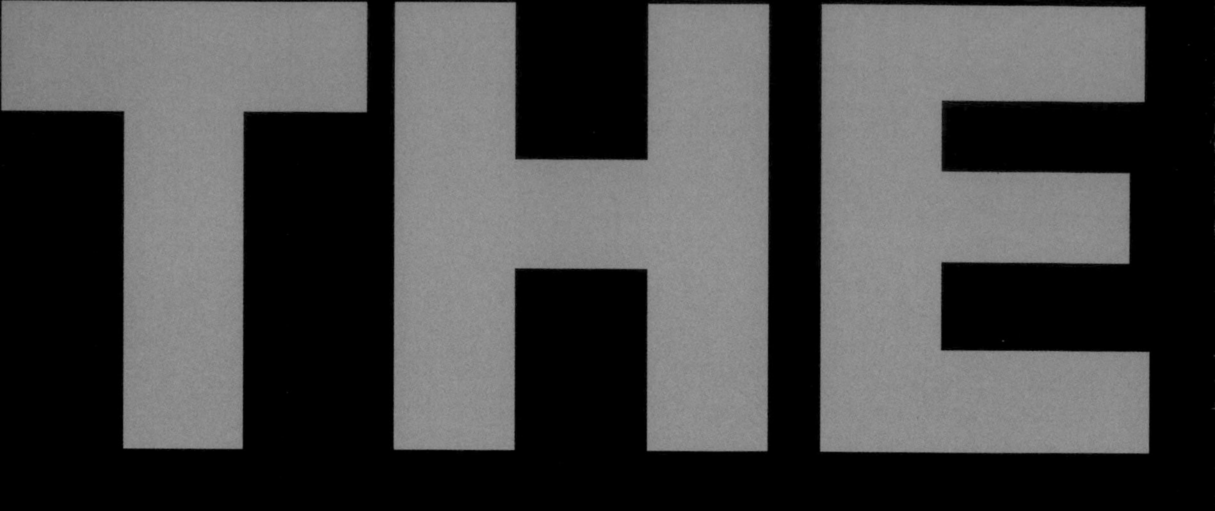
THE

# FIX

--AND THEN DETECTIVE BRUNDO GRABBED THE SUSPECT'S WEAPON WITH HIS LEFT HAND, JUST AS IT WAS BEING FIRED--BUT MANAGED TO HOLD ONTO IT EVEN AS THE BULLET IMPACTED WITH BARE HAND, THUS SAVING COUNTLESS LIVES--

DO YOU DIPSHITS EVEN HEAR YOUR-SELVES?
I CAN ONLY DESCRIBE WHAT I SAW, SHERYL.
AND WHAT I SAW WAS A HERO.
YOU SHOT YOUR GODDAMNED PARTNER IN THE HAND, ROY.

ARE YOU SAYING I'M THE MASKED FLAG-BURNER? 'CAUSE THAT DOESN'T EVEN MAKE SENSE. READ THE REPORT AGAIN, IT SAYS I JUDO-KICKED HIM A BUNCH OF TIMES. UNLESS YOU'RE SAYING HE'S A CLONE OF ME, WHICH WOULD BE AWESOME...
I PRESUME YOU HAVE WITNESSES TO ALL THIS?

WELL, NOT TO THE HELICOPTER CHASE--BUT THE LAST PART?
SURE, WE GOT A COUPLE HOMELESS GUYS.
AND WHAT ABOUT THE BUS FULL OF--WHAT DOES IT SAY HERE--HOT NUNS THAT YOU SAVED?

DIDN'T WANNA TESTIFY.
ROY, I TOLD YOU TO FAKE AN INJURY. FALL DOWN SOME STAIRS.

NOBODY MAKES A MOVIE ABOUT GUYS FALLING DOWN STAIRS, SHERYL. BUT A MASKED FLAG-BURNING TERRORIST IN A HELICOPTER THAT TARGETS SEXY WOMEN OF THE CLOTH ON A BUS?
THAT'S SPEED MEETS SISTER ACT MEETS AIRWOLF!

YOU'RE AN IDIOT.
YEAH, YOU'RE PROBABLY RIGHT. NOBODY REALLY REMEMBERS AIRWOLF...
THIS IS GONNA TAKE EVERYTHING I GOT TO COVER OVER...
...JOSH WANTED YOU TO KEEP A LOW PROFILE, REMEMBER?
TRUST ME--

"HE IS NOT GONNA BE HAPPY ABOUT THIS."
CHEW
MAIL POUCH
TOBACCO

BOUNCE BOUNCE
BOUNCE BOUNCE
Bill MONROE
WSM

BOUNCE BOUNCE
BOUNCE BOUNCE
MAIL POUCH
XXX

AH--I'M REALLY SORRY, FELLAS-- I DO HAVE TO TAKE THIS. BUT-- GREAT JOB ALL AROUND--TOBY, I THINK YOU WERE COMING IN A LITTLE FLAT ON THE HARMONY THERE AT THE END.
WAS I?
AH, MAYBE JUST MY EAR. LET'S BREAK FOR A COUPLE, THEN COME BACK WITH LOVE WILL TEAR US APART.

OH HI, SHERYL! YES, I DID GET YOUR MESSAGE, SORRY, ME AND THE REST OF THE GUYS WERE JUST HIP DEEP IN A REAL JAM SESSION, YOU KNOW? SEEING WHERE THE BLUE-GRASS TAKES US.

SORRY? WAIT--HE WHAT?

I'MMA BOUT TO TAKE MY KEY, STICK IT IN THE IG--
MONROE

STILL...
MONROE

FUCKING...
MONROE
WSM

FLAT!
WIND WIND WIND

Bill
MONRO
BLUE G
WSM GRAND OL

BANJO PLAYER WANTED!
OVER-30 BLUEGRASS GROUP.
SPECIALIZES IN NEW WAVE & PUNK COVERS - ESP. JOY DIVISION

EH, I'M SURE IT'LL BE FINE.
SHERYL MALONE INTERNAL AFFAIRS

BESIDES, HE SHOULD BE HAPPY, WE'RE TAKING REAL, POSITIVE STEPS TO ADDRESS OUR MONETARY OBLIGATIONS.
HOLE IN THE HAND POSITIVE.
YOU SHOULD KNOW, HE WAS DOING DISGUSTING, UNNATURAL THINGS WITH THAT HAND. AND NOW HE HAS THE PERFECT REASON TO REQUEST A TEMPORARY TRANSFER WHILE HE RECUPERATES.

AND WHILE WE'RE ON THE SUBJECT OF DEBTS AND NEW CAREER OPPORTUNITIES-- WHILE I HATE TO BRING THIS UP--PAYING JOSH OFF HAS BEEN A REAL BURDEN ON ME, FINANCIALLY--
YOU HAVEN'T ACTUALLY PAID HIM BACK ANYTHING.

RIGHT, BUT THE STRESS OF IT HAS REALLY PUT A DAMPER ON MY PRODUCTIVITY! WHICH MEANS I COULD REALLY USE SOME OFF-DUTY OVERTIME.
I GUESS YOU SHOULD TALK TO YOUR DEPARTMENT HEAD.
RIGHT, BUT MY DEPARTMENT ISN'T ALWAYS TRYING TO SLEEP WITH ME...

=SIGH= --FINE. I KNOW THERE'S SOME OPENINGS AT PASEO DE LA PLAZA, DURING THIS TACO FESTIVAL THING--
WHAT? NO, NO--I MEAN A GOOD SECURITY DETAIL. A REAL V.I.P. NEEDING SOME POLICE PROTECTION--AND WILLING TO PAY THE DOUBLE TIME THAT COMES WITH IT.
TAPTAPTAPTAPTAPTAPTAPTAP
I SUPPOSE YOU HAD SOMEONE IN MIND?

YOU'RE SO FUCKING PREDICTABLE, ROY. I WISH I COULD HELP, BUT I KNOW FOR A FACT THAT GIG'S ALREADY TAKEN--
WHAT? BY WHO?

PETE.
160 W.P.M.

PETE DANIELSON.
PETE DANIELSON IS THE **NICEST** GUY.

PETE DANIELSON KISSES HIS WIFE GOODBYE EVERY MORNING, BEFORE DRIVING THEIR TWO BEAUTIFUL GIRLS TO SCHOOL.
#1 MOM

PETE DANIELSON ALWAYS BRINGS DONUTS TO WORK, EVERY THURSDAY. AND NOT THE CHEAP, SHITTY KIND--

HE DRIVES FORTY MINUTES AGAINST RUSH HOUR TRAFFIC TO GET THEM FROM PRIMO'S IN SAWTELLE.

WHERE HE ALWAYS LEAVES A TIP IN THE JAR.

PETE DANIELSON FIXES OLD ABANDONED CARS ON THE WEEKENDS, THEN GIVES THE PROCEEDS FROM THEIR SALES TO CHARITIES FOR DEAF AND BLIND KIDS.

PETE DANIELSON TAKES A MICROCHIP SCANNER WITH HIM TO GRIFFITH PARK ONCE A MONTH, CHECKING STRAY CATS FOR MICRO-CHIPS SO THAT HE CAN RETURN THEM TO THEIR OWNERS.

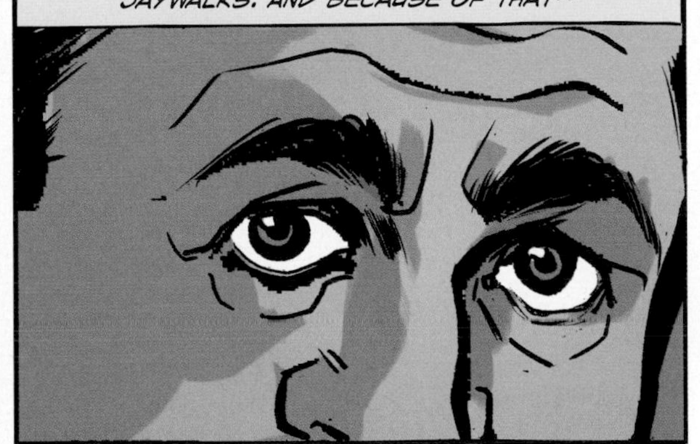
PETE DANIELSON HAS NEVER MISSED AN ELECTION, ATTENDS CHURCH SERVICES WEEKLY, NEVER, EVER JAYWALKS. AND BECAUSE OF THAT--

I AM GOING TO DESTROY YOU TODAY, PETE DANIELSON.

I CAN'T SEE ME LOVIN NOBODY BUT YOU--
PRIMO'S

SNIFF SNIFF SNIFF

UM... HELLO?

ROY! NO!
ROY-- WHAT--WHAT WERE YOU DOING?!
PETE?!
WERE YOU ABOUT TO--

YES! YES, I WAS GONNA END IT ALL, OKAY! I DIDN'T THINK ANYONE WOULD BE HERE THIS EARLY.
WHAT ELSE AM I SUPPOSED TO DO?! I'M GONNA LOSE MY JOB, PETE! THEY'RE GONNA TAKE MY BADGE!
WHOA... SLOW DOWN, BUDDY--WHAT HAPPENED?

I'M LAST ON THE BOARD--YOU KNOW THAT, RIGHT? BEEN MONTHS SINCE I CRACKED A HOMICIDE INVESTIGATION.
WELL, SURE, I HEARD SOME GUYS TALKING, BUT--WE ALL HIT SLUMPS, ROY.
YESTERDAY, CAPTAIN CALLS ME IN--TELLS ME CITY HALL'S PUSHING CUTBACKS, SAYS HE'S GOTTA LET SOMEONE GO.

OH NO...
SO I BEGGED... I PLEADED--AND HE SAID HE'D GIVE ME ONE MORE CHANCE.
WELL, HEY THERE, YOU GO--
NO, YOU DON'T UNDERSTAND! HE SAID IF I WANTED TO KEEP MY JOB--

MADIGAN, Y
"I'D HAVE TO CLOSE THE MADIGAN FILE!"

VINCE MADIGAN. FOUND IN HIS STUDIO APARTMENT, ALONE, SHOT THREE TIMES AND BACK OF THE HEAD TRAUMA.
HE WAS UNEMPLOYED, WITH NO REAL FRIENDS OR FAMILY.
NO CRIMINAL RECORD, NO DEBTS, AND NO ONE CONNECTED TO HIM WITH ANY MOTIVE TO KILL.
NO DNA OR FORENSIC EVIDENCE, NO SIGN OF A STRUGGLE OR FORCED ENTRY.
IT IS AN ICE-COLD CASE. PLACED ON THREE DESKS IN SIX WEEKS, ITS ONLY PURPOSE IS TO DRAG DOWN A DETECTIVE'S CLOSING RATE.
IT IS, QUITE SIMPLY, AN UNSOLVABLE MURDER.
MIGHT AS WELL JUST SAVE EVERYONE THE TROUBLE--
WHOA, WHOA, HOLD ON THERE, BUDDY--
DON'T GIVE UP SO FAST. MAYBE, TOGETHER, WE COULD COME UP WITH SOMETHING. COUPLE'A FRESH EYES ON THIS THING CAN'T HURT, RIGHT?
YOU MEAN, YOU'D-- SNIFF --HELP ME?
OF COURSE I WOULD!
SIGH I APPRECIATE IT, PETE, BUT--IT WOULDN'T MATTER. IF CAPTAIN FOUND OUT I WAS PULLING YOU OFF YOUR OWN CASE LOAD TO BAIL ME OUT--
HEY NOW...
WHO SAYS CAPTAIN HAS TO FIND OUT?
YES SIR, THAT PETE DANIELSON, HE SURE LOVES TO HELP--

SO THAT'S EXACTLY WHAT HE DOES.
HE MOVES TOWARDS ME--
THEN I SHOOT HIM THREE TIMES...
HE STUMBLES THREE STEPS BACK, FALLS HERE...

ROY, IT LOOKS LIKE YOUR FILES HERE ARE BLOCKED--
NO WORRIES, JUST USE MY PASSWORD--
"JIZZMOTRONSUX75"

YOU KNOW, NOW THAT I THINK ABOUT IT--I DO REMEMBER HEARING SOMEBODY DIGGING AROUND IN THE BACK THAT NIGHT--

YOU CAN SEE WHERE THE BULLET GOES THROUGH HERE...
POOR GUY.

MAN, IT WAS HOT UP THERE, RIGHT?
HERE YA GO, YA BIG SWEATY LUG.
THANKS--WHEN I RETIRE, IT'S GONNA BE TO SOME PLACE COLD, YA KNOW?

I CAN'T BELIEVE WE'RE RIGHT BACK WHERE WE STARTED--
HOW IS THAT EVEN POSSIBLE?
I'M SORRY I WASN'T MORE HELP, ROY--THIS REALLY IS A TOUGH ONE--

I WISH THERE WAS MORE I COULD DO TO HELP.
HEY, YOU TRIED, PAL, THAT'S ALL THAT--
WAIT, HOLD ON A SEC--
THAT'S IT!

I GOT IT!
THAT'S RIGHT--

WHO'S A GREAT DETECTIVE?
HERE COMES THE AEROPLANE-- V-RROOOOM--
MMM!

KNOCK KNOCK!

HOW'S MY HERO COP PARTNER DOING?
THIS SOUP IS COLD.
HEY--WAS THAT--WAS THAT YOUR NURSE?

NURSE GRANDPA-FUCKER?
AW, MAN, DON'T CALL HER THAT...
WHY ELSE WOULD YOU WORK THERE?

NOW, COME ON...SHOW ME.
DUDE--
SHOW ME.

WOW... LOOK AT THAT, BUDDY. WENT CLEAN THROUGH. YOU KNOW, YOU WERE WORRIED ABOUT BEING ABLE TO JERK OFF WITH IT, BUT NOW YOU GOT A NICE HOLE TO WORK WITH.
WHAT ARE YOU TALKING ABOUT? I CAN'T EVEN FIT MY PINKIE THROUGH IT.
THAT'S ALSO TRUE.

THING IS, DOC SAYS WITH THE NERVE DAMAGE, I MIGHT NOT BE ABLE TO USE THE HAND AT ALL ANYMORE...
WELL, YOU KNEW THE RISKS GOING IN, BUDDY. BUT GOOD NEWS IS, YOUR TRANSFER PAPERWORK HAS BEEN FAST-TRACKED, AND I THINK--

OOH, TURN IT UP! I'M ON!
SHOCKING NEWS IN AN UNSOLVED MURDER CASE THIS EVENING--

AS A LOS ANGELES POLICE DEPARTMENT HOMICIDE DETECTIVE HAS BEEN ARRESTED IN CONNECTION TO THE SLAYING OF FIFTY-SIX-YEAR-OLD VINCE MADIGAN.
INVESTIGATORS SAY THEY WERE STUNNED BY THE DEVELOPMENT--

I'VE KNOWN PETE DANIELSON FOR YEARS.
HE IS AS GOOD A MAN AS I'VE EVER KNOWN--A PILLAR IN THE COMMUNITY.
I JUST... I CAN'T BELIEVE IT'S TRUE.

CAN YOU TELL US A LITTLE BIT ABOUT WHAT LED YOU TO THE DISCOVERY, DETECTIVE.
WELL, AS THE OFFICER TASKED WITH SOLVING THE MADIGAN CASE, I FIRST BECAME SUSPICIOUS WHEN I FOUND OUT DETECTIVE DANIELSON HAD BEEN LOGGING IN TO OUR SYSTEM, UNDER MY USER I.D. TO ALTER EVIDENCE DOCUMENTATION.

YUP.

THIS PROMPTED ME TO TAKE A FRESH LOOK AT THE CRIME SCENE, WHERE WE FOUND NEW DNA EVIDENCE MATCHES TO DANIELSON--

YUP.

I THEN CONFRONTED HIM, AT WHICH POINT, HE IMMEDIATELY CONFESSED.
THEN I SHOOT HIM THREE TIMES...
AND THEN HE GAVE US THE LOCATION OF THE MURDER WEAPON, WHICH WAS COVERED IN FINGERPRINT MATCHES FOR DANIELSON, OBVIOUSLY.

YUUUUUP.

BUT IN SPITE OF HIS EARLIER CONFESSION, DANIELSON STRUCK A DEFIANT TONE WHEN TAKEN INTO CUSTODY.
IT WASN'T ME!
THIS IS A SETUP!
IT WAS ROY! ROY, I'LL KILL YOU FOR THIS, YOU LYING MOTHERFUCKER!
WHICH YOU MIGHT THINK PEOPLE WOULD BELIEVE. BUT FUNNY ENOUGH--

THERE'S A REASON PETE'S WIFE DOESN'T LOOK TERRIBLY UPSET ABOUT ALL THIS.

#1 MOM

OR WHY THE GUY'S CO-WORKERS REALLY DON'T SEEM SO SURPRISED.

HELL, DONUT LADY CAN PROBABLY SUM IT UP BEST--
HA! I KNEW IT!

IT DIDN'T HURT WHEN THEY FOUND ALL THAT STUFF WHEN THEY SEARCHED PETE'S HOUSE.

AND SURE, NOW IT'D BE FAIR IF YOU ASKED--ROY, DID YOU PLANT SOMETHING AT THE GUY'S HOUSE?!
MAYBE, MAYBE NOT. BUT I BET YOU I DIDN'T HAVE TO, EITHER WAY. SEE, HERE'S THE THING--

EVERYONE HAS SOMETHING ON THEIR COMPUTER. OR IN THEIR TRUNK. OR BURIED IN THE BACK-YARD. TRUST ME, AS A COP, I SEE IT EVERY SINGLE TIME.
AND SO IF YOU'RE **SMART**, YOU KEEP YOUR HEAD DOWN, TRY NOT TO DRAW TOO MUCH ATTENTION TO YOURSELF, AND KEEP YOUR MOUTH SHUT WHEN SOMEONE **ELSE** IS GETTING BURNED AT THE STAKE.

BUT GUYS LIKE PETE, RUNNING AROUND BEING NICE TO EVERYONE, PLAYING IT OH-SO-RESPECTABLE AND MAKING A BIG SHOW OF IT-- LET ME TELL YOU WHAT THAT **REALLY** MEANS--

IT MEANS WHATEVER THEY'VE GOT HIDDEN? IT SCARES THE SHIT OUT OF THEM SO BADLY THAT THEY CAN'T KEEP THEMSELVES FROM **OVERCOMPENSATING**.

YOU CAN **SMELL** IT ON THEM--THAT DESPERATE NEED FOR YOU TO LOOK PAST THEM, TO ELIMINATE THEM FROM SUSPICION. TO GET THAT "YES, YOU'RE ONE OF THE GOOD ONES" NOD.
TRUTH IS, THEY'RE DOING THE MATH ON THEIR OWN HUMANITY, AND FINDING THEMSELVES SO FAR IN THE NEGATIVE THEY GOTTA GO FULL-ON **MOTHER TERESA** JUST TO BALANCE THE BOOKS.
30
22
POP

SERIOUSLY, IF I GIVE YOU ONE PIECE OF ADVICE THAT YOU LISTEN TO, LET IT BE THIS--
POLICE
5' 9"
5' 6"
5' 3"
POLIC
NEVER, **EVER** TRUST THE NICEST GUY IN THE ROOM.

WHEN YOU'RE WITH ME, BABY, THE SKIES WILL BE BLUE--

YOU READY TO GO?
AND SURE I'LL ADMIT, I WAS HOPING FOR A **WARMER** WELCOME.
AFTER ALL, IT'S LIKE THEY SAY--

--FIRST IMPRESSIONS ARE EVERYTHING.
DETECTIVE BRUNDO?

HI, I'M OFFICER RYAN.
OH, HEY, NICE TO MEET YA--

OH, GOSH, LOOK AT THAT.
AH, IT'S NOTHIN'--
LOS ANGELES AIRPORT POLICE

WHAT DO YOU MEAN NOTHING? I HEARD ALL ABOUT IT! WHAT WAS IT LIKE, FLYING ONE OF THOSE HELICOPTERS?
UH-- HEROIC. REAL HEROIC.
I BET. SO--

YOU READY TO MEET YOUR NEW PARTNER?

HE'S A BIG DEAL HERO COP, TOO, YOU KNOW.
OH YEAH, I--KNOW.
YOU OKAY THERE, DETECTIVE BRUNDO?
SURE, YEAH--JUST NERVOUS.
I DID THAT THING WHERE YOU RUB TURKEY BACON ALL OVER YOUR HANDS, I GOT A COUPLE TREATS IN EACH OF MY POCKETS--

I JUST REALLY WANNA MAKE SURE HE LIKES ME.
AW, I DON'T THINK YOU NEED TO WORRY. NO MATTER WHAT THEY SAY, HE'S A BIG OL' SOFTIE.
GOT A NOSE FOR THE CRIMINALS, BUT EVERYONE ELSE HE'S--
BARK BARK

HMPH. HE'S JUST UP AHEAD--
BARK BARK BARK BARK
THAT'S WEIRD. NEVER REALLY SEEN HIM ACT LIKE THIS BEFORE...
BARK BARK
OH, WELL-- BEST OF LUCK TO YOU FELLAS!
BARK-BARK-BARK-BARK
AND THERE YOU GO. SEE? THAT WASN'T SO BAD.
YOU WERE PROMISED A DOG--
BARK BARK BARK BARK BARK BARK
BARK BARK BARK BARK BARK BARK BARK

BARK BARK BARK BARK BARK
YOU GOT A DOG.

IT STARTS OFF INNOCENTLY ENOUGH...

YOU'VE GOT A KID THAT LIKES BEING IN FRONT OF THE CAMERA--
CHOO
REC
AND PARENTS WHO LIKE MAKING MONEY OFF HER.

SO THEY ENROLL HER IN A BUNCH OF TALENT COMPETITIONS AND BEAUTY PAGEANTS--
THAT GETS THEM IN THE DOOR AT AUDITIONS.

AND THAT'S WHERE THE RECORD DEAL COMES IN. THE TEENAGE YEARS, PART ONE--THE STARLIGHT SISTERS. NOT ACTUALLY SISTERS, NOT ACTUALLY TALENTED MUSICIANS. THAT'S THE TWIST.
BUT IT IS ENOUGH TO GET A CERTAIN ROCK ROLLING DOWNHILL--

FAST FORWARD A COUPLE YEARS, AND THE FIRST "LEAKED" SELFIE DROPS.

AFTER THAT, HALF THE COUNTRY IS WATCHING A COUNTDOWN CLOCK TO SEE WHAT HAPPENS WHEN THE BARELY GETS DROPPED OFF THE LEGAL.
AND THE CUSTOMER IS ALWAYS RIGHT. THE MUSIC NOW INVOLVES A POLE SOMEHOW. THE VIDEOS ARE PRIMARILY WATCHED ON MUTE. IN INTERVIEWS, SHE TELLS US HOW SHE'S "DISCOVERING HER SEXUALITY" AND "LETTING IT ALL OUT."

SO THEY PUT HER IN ONE OF THOSE 8PM FAMILY SITCOMS: LIKE **I WOOF YOU**--THE STORY OF THE SPECIAL BOND BETWEEN A LITTLE GIRL AND HER TALKING DOG.

OF COURSE, THERE'S NO POINT IN PUTTING ALL THIS WORK IN UNLESS YOU'RE TRYING TO SELL SOMETHING--

--TAKE THEM FOR ROLLING STONE, YOU JUST SAVED THE PUBLISHING INDUSTRY. BIGGEST-SELLING ISSUE OF THE YEAR. BY A LOT.

SHE'S STILL ACTING, KINDA--MOSTLY IN LOW-BUDGET WITH ARTHOUSE DIRECTORS, THOUGH. SO ARTHOUSE THEY USUALLY INVOLVE PARTIAL NUDITY AND SOME SERIOUS GIRL ON GIRL. BUT IT DOESN'T MATTER--SHE DOESN'T NEED TO WORK TO BE FAMOUS ANYMORE.

NO, PRIMARILY SHE EXISTS AS THE LATEST IN A PROUD LINEAGE THAT DEFINES MODERN-DAY AMERICA--A DYNASTY MORE POWERFUL THAN THE KENNEDYS, CLINTONS, AND BUSHES PUT TOGETHER--THAT'S RIGHT--

I'M TALKING ABOUT CHILDREN GROOMED BY MULTIBILLION DOLLAR CORPORATIONS TO SOMEDAY GIVE US SOMETHING TO JERK OFF TO.

OH GOD YEAH, I WOULD SO FUCK HER.

I FIGURED.
I HEARD SHE FUCKED THAT DOG.
THE I WOOF YOU DOG? THAT'S PRETTY MESSED UP, DONOVAN.
NAH, IT'S NOT BESTIALITY IF THE DOG CAN TALK, DUDE.
BUT YOU'RE RIGHT, THIS IS GOOD NEWS!

EXACTLY! I FIGURE THIS THE PERFECT OPPORTUNITY --I EARN HER TRUST, BUILD A RAPPORT--
LET ME KNOW IF YOU NEED ANY HELP BUILDING IT, I'M VERY COCK-SAVVY AND I DON'T MIND A LITTLE DRIP DOWN. ACTUALLY KINDA SOOTHING.

--THEN EVENTUALLY I TELL HER ABOUT THIS OPTION DEAL I HAVE WITH YOU. I MEAN, YOU'RE ALWAYS SAYING HOW MUCH IT HELPS TO GET A BIG NAME ATTACHED YOUR PROJECT, AND SHE'S HUGE.
HUGE LIKE THE BONER SHE GIVES ME.

YEAH, JUST LIKE YOUR BONER. THING IS--I'VE GOT A PLAN, BUT--I DON'T HAVE ANYTHING TO SHOW HER. I MEAN, WE DON'T HAVE A SCRIPT YET...
WE DON'T NEED ONE.
WE'LL JUST DO A TREATMENT.
WHAT'S THAT?

IT'S WHERE YOU JUST WRITE DOWN ALL THE STUFF THAT HAPPENS IN THE MOVIE.
LIKE A SCRIPT.
NAH, I MEAN WITHOUT ALL THE DIALOG AND THE BORING SHIT.
SO LIKE AN OUTLINE?
NO, MORE LIKE YOU'RE TELLING THE STORY.
MORE DETAIL, YOU KNOW?

SEEMS POINTLESS--WHY WOULDN'T YOU JUST GET SOMEONE TO WRITE A SCRIPT?
EH, UNION RULES, YOU GOTTA PAY WRITERS FOR SCRIPTS. TREATMENT'S BASICALLY A WAY TO GET A WRITER TO WRITE YOUR WHOLE MOVIE, BUT FOR WAY LESS MONEY.

AND THEY GO FOR THAT?
OF COURSE THEY GO FOR THAT, ROY, THEY'RE FUCKING WRITERS! LISTEN, MAN--WAIT, HOLD ON--

UH... DONOVAN? YOU OKAY?

HNNK.

DID YOU JUST--
THANKS, LENORE! PICK YOURSELF UP A DIET SPRITE ON THE WAY OUT--IT'S ON ME.

DID YOU JUST GET A FUCKING BLOWJOB UNDER THE TABLE?
YEAH?

WE WERE TALKING THE WHOLE TIME--JESUS CHRIST, YOU WERE LOOKING RIGHT AT ME!
WHAT? YOU'VE GOT KIND EYES.

THAT'S FUCKING DISGUSTING, DONOVAN!
IT'S FOR MY ANXIETY! I HAVE A PRESCRIPTION.
I CAN'T EVEN--
OKAY, OKAY, RIGHT--I GET WHAT THIS IS ABOUT--

NEXT TIME I'LL SHARE. I PROMISE.
AND YEAH, THIS IS A BUMPY START TO THE DAY, BUT TRUST ME--

IT GETS A LOT WORSE.

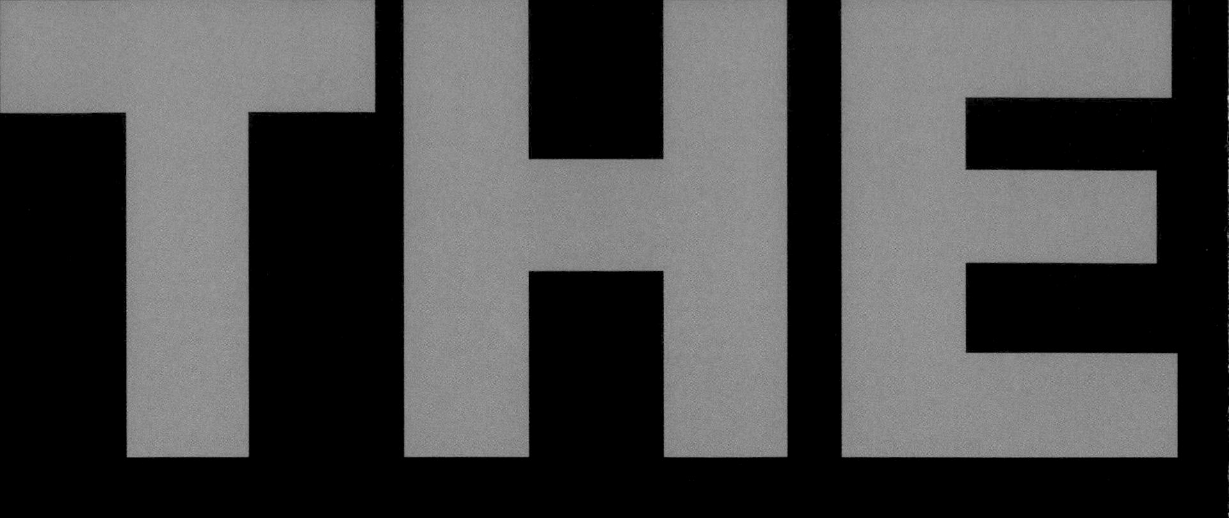
THE

FIX
SIGH
Buying Forclosed Properties
ASSHOLES
by Dr. Maxon Arboghast
SALE 1195

LET'S GO THEN.

AFTER YOU, MILADY...
JESUS, WHY IS YOUR CAR SO OLD?
THE TERM IS VINTAGE, I BELIEVE.

...WHERE ARE THE DONUTS?
SORRY?
PETE ALWAYS BROUGHT ME DONUTS. YOU KNOW WHAT HAPPENS TO MY BLOOD SUGAR IF I DON'T EAT?

YOU TURN INTO A MASSIVE BITCH?
YOU GET DROWSY?
YEAH, DROWSY.
GOING THROUGH GLOVE COMPARTMENT

SURE--WELL, IT BEING VINTAGE, I TRY TO LIMIT EATING IN THE CAR. YOU KNOW, TO PROTECT THE INTERIOR. BUT NOW I KNOW FOR NEXT TIME--DONUTS.
FROM PRIMO'S.
GOOD OL' PRIMO'S.

IS PETE OKAY? I MEAN, I SAW IT ON THE NEWS. THERE'S NO WAY HE KILLED THAT GUY, HE'S A TOTAL PUSSY.
I HEAR YA. IT'S A REAL TRAVESTY OF JUSTICE.
HAVE YOU BEEN TO SEE HIM?
HUH? OH, SURE, SURE. PUT MY NIPPLE UP TO THE GLASS AND EVERYTHING--

"HE'S DOING GREAT."
OOOHHH GAAWWDDD... WHYYYYY...
FAP
FAP
FAP

LIKE I GIVE A SHIT. COME ON, WE GOTTA GET GOING--

LET'S BE *CLEAR* HERE, ALL RIGHT?

YOU DO NOT GET TO ACCIDENTALLY BRUSH MY TITS.

YOU DO NOT GET TO ACCIDENTALLY BRUSH MY *FRIEND'S* TITS.

I WILL COVER YOUR BAR TAB...
¢

...BUT YOU'RE DRINKING WELL, NOT CALL, GOT IT?
$

WE WILL NOT BE TAKING A PICTURE TOGETHER.

IT CAN BE HARD TO TELL BETWEEN THE AGENTS AND THE PEDOPHILES, BUT THAT IS LIKE NINE-TENTHS OF THE JOB.
A

PETE WAS A DIPSHIT BUT HE HAD A REAL GIFT FOR THIS, I GUESS BECAUSE HE WAS THE LAST MAN IN AMERICA THAT ENJOYED FUCKING HIS WIFE.
P

SO NOW YOU ENJOY FUCKING YOUR WIFE, UNDERSTAND?

I'M ACTUALLY NOT MARRIED.
AND FROM THERE--

THINGS ACTUALLY GO PRETTY WELL.
I MEAN, WHO CAN COMPLAIN ABOUT A GIG LIKE THIS, RIGHT?

YOU GET TO STAND SLIGHTLY TO THE SIDE OF THE BEST TABLES IN THE HOTTEST CLUBS IN HOLLYWOOD, DRINKING OVERPRICED WHISKEY! THAT'S RIGHT, EVEN THE WELL IS CRAZY OVERPRICED!
THIS IS WHAT I WAS MADE FOR.

NO MORE SPENDING MY LIFE IN THE GUTTER, MINGLING WITH PEASANTS. I WAS BUILT FOR SOMETHING BETTER--THESE ARE MY PEOPLE.

BUT THEN JUST AS I'M REALLY STARTING TO GET COMFORTABLE IN MY NEWFOUND PERIPHERAL CELEBRITY, I REMEMBER--

FAME COMES WITH ONE HELL OF A DOWNSIDE.
...THE FUCK?
PULL OVER!

TOBIAS!
OH HI, ELAINA--
HEY. THOUGHT YOU WERE STAYING IN TONIGHT.

YOU KNOW, I WAS GOING TO--BUT THEN RITA HERE CONVINCED ME OTHERWISE. SHE'S A PERSUASIVE LADY.
MM. SO WE ARE STILL ON FOR WEDNESDAY, THEN?

I WISH. RESHOOTS.
YOU KNOW HOW IT IS, BABE.
I DO--

I REALLY DO.

LET'S GO.
EVERYTHING OKAY?

OH SURE--
LONG AS YOU'RE COOL.
AND AS WE HIT THE SECOND ACT BOTTOM, I CAN'T SAY I'M ALL THAT SURPRISED.

SEE, THIS IS THE WEIRDEST PART OF THE WHOLE "CHILD STAR TURNED SEX FANTASY" THING.

IT NEVER ENDS WELL FOR THEM.

THE PROBLEM IS THE DIMINISHING RETURNS.
HOOD
RIVER
Tastes like

SEE, THOSE FIRST FEW YEARS, EVERY LITTLE FLASH OF SKIN OR TEASING SMILE IS LIKE A RELEASE ON A PRESSURE VALVE.

BUT ONCE IT'S OUT THERE IN THE OPEN, AND ONCE IT'S ALLOWED--

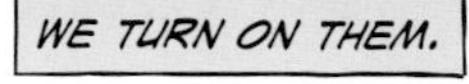
WE TURN ON THEM.

AND THINGS GET UGLY.

THE WORLD IS A CRUEL PLACE--BUT NEVER CRUELER THAN A GUY MASTURBATING TO A MUSIC VIDEO WHILE CALLING THE SINGER A WHORE IN THE YOUTUBE COMMENTS.
PAPARAZZI CHASE, GOSSIP SITES RIDICULE; THE HIGH-MINDED JUST SCOFF. FRIENDS ARE REPLACED WITH HANGERS-ON. POINT IS--DON'T GO ONLINE.

THEN AGAIN, I GUESS THIS SHOULD ALL BE EXPECTED.
AFTER ALL, THE WHOLE THING WAS BUILT ON SOME QUEASY, WINK-AND-NOD FORBIDDEN FRUIT BULLSHIT. IT WAS ALL SO ALLURING.
BUT THEN THEY GAVE US WHAT WE WANTED--

--AND THERE'S NOTHING MORE UNATTRACTIVE THAN THAT.

BASICALLY IT'S INEVITABLE, THEN, THAT AT AGE NINETEEN, THIS KIND OF BACKLASH CAUSES THE GIRL IN QUESTION TO BREAK DOWN IN A CLUSTER-FUCK OF DESIGNER DRUGS AND BOOZE. I'M NOT ONE TO JUDGE. STILL, THOUGH--

PROBABLY WASN'T A GOOD IDEA TO GIVE HER MY GUN.
NOW, ELAINA--I DON'T THINK YOU WANT TO--

SHUT THE FUCK UP, COP!
YOU DON'T KNOW ME! YOU DON'T KNOW MY SHIT!

IT'S TRUE, I'VE ONLY BEEN ACQUAINTED WITH YOUR SHIT FOR A FEW HOURS, BUT--
I'M PRETTY SURE YOU DON'T WANT TO KILL ANYONE...

YEAH? THIS LOOK LIKE I DON'T WANNA KILL ANYONE?!

FUCK IT. I BLOW MY OWN BRAINS OUT--

I JUST MAKE THE HATERS HAPPY.

TWITTER'D GO APESHIT.

BE THE ONLY THING PEOPLE'VE SEEN OF MINE SINCE HIGH SCHOOL BITCHES 3.

SIGH-- LET'S GO HOME.

APESHIT!

HUH?
OH, COME ON, YOU'RE SUPPOSED TO BE A DETECTIVE. TOBIAS IS GAY. OBVIOUSLY. I'M HIS DIE HARD REBOOT.
HIS WHAT?

YOU KNOW, THE GIRL AN ACTOR PRETENDS TO BE FUCKING SO THAT HE CAN BE CAST IN THE LEAD OF A DIE HARD REBOOT.
IS THAT ACTUALLY A THING THAT'S HAPPENING?
WHAT? THE DIE HARD THING OR THE SHAMEFULLY REPRESSIVE SUBCULTURE?
DOESN'T MATTER. I GUESS YOU'RE FINE THEN?

BUT I'M COUNTING IT AS A BONDING EXPERIENCE.
SHE WON'T FORGET THE COP THAT WAS THERE FOR HER IN HER DARKEST HOUR, ASSUMING SHE REMEMBERS ANY OF THIS.

THEN AGAIN, MAYBE THE NIGHT'S ABOUT TO GET A LOT MORE MEMORABLE.

DID YOU?
NO...

AND I SET THE ALARM.

WAIT HERE.

OKAY, ELAINA, I THINK IT'S SAFE FOR YOU TO--
I DON'T *FUCKING* BELIEVE THIS!

I BEEN *BLING RINGED!*

THEY TOOK MY JEWELRY AND MY GOOD JEWELRY... *FUCKING ASSHOLES!*
*OH,* THIS IS JUST... TERRIBLE. BUT--DON'T YOU WORRY, ELAINA. I AM GOING TO FIND *WHOEVER* WAS RESPONSIBLE FOR THIS--

I AM GOING TO FIND THEM AND BRING THEM TO *JUSTICE.*
NOW, I'LL FILE A REPORT, THEN GO TO MY COMMANDING OFFICER AND TELL HIM I *DEMAND* TO BE PUT IN CHARGE OF THE INVESTIGATION, BUT IN THE MEANTIME I'LL LEAVE YOU MY NUMBER--
*HM,* DIDN'T BRING MY *CARDS* AND I DON'T SEEM TO HAVE ANYTHING TO WRITE MY NUMBER ON--

OH WAIT! YES, I DO--

THIS IS JUST A LITTLE *PRE-WRITE* TREATMENT I HAD DONE WITH THE FOLKS AT UNICORN PICTURES, IT'S BASED ON THE TIME MY PARTNER AND I TOOK ON A *MASTER THIEF* WHO WAS ATTACKING THE ELDERLY.

HEY, YOU KNOW, I HADN'T REALLY THOUGHT ABOUT IT BEFORE, BUT--THERE MIGHT BE A PART IN HERE YOU'D BE PERFECT FOR. HAVE YOU EVER WANTED TO PLAY A NUN?

ARE YOU *FUCKING* SERIOUS?
I JUST GOT *ROBBED* AND YOU'RE TRYING TO GIVE ME YOUR *SHITTY* SCRIPT?!
WHAT GAVE AWAY THAT IT WAS SHITTY?

*OKAY, BIT OF A HICCUP THERE AS WELL. BUT THERE'S ALWAYS--*
*GET THE FUCK OUT!*

ONE HOUR LATER.
RING RING
'YELLO.
ROY?! ROY, IT'S ELAINA--
OH WOW, DID YOU READ IT ALREADY?
NOW BEFORE YOU SAY ANYTHING, I KNOW THE SCENE WHERE I'M RIDING THE ELEPHANT NEEDS WORK--
99¢ TACOS
JACK IN THE BOX

SHUT UP! SHUT UP-- SOMEBODY'S IN THE HOUSE--
HUH?

THE GUYS WHO BROKE IN--I THINK THEY'RE BACK! I CAN HEAR THEM. WHAT DO I DO?

OKAY, DON'T WORRY--I'M ON MY WAY! JUST--JUST HIDE IN A CLOSET UNTIL I GET THERE--

OH FUCK, I CAN HEAR THEM, THEY'RE OUT IN THE HALL--
ELAINA?!
OH MY GOD! NO! NO! AYYEEE! ROY--

ELAINA--HOLD ON! I'M COMING!

WELL, THIS IS UNEXPECTED.

ELAINA?!
WHO THE FUCK IS THAT?!

WHO THE FUCK ARE YOU?

...WE ASKED FIRST!

I'M A COP, ASSHOLES.

BUT I'M NOT TECHNICALLY ON DUTY!

PUT THE GUN ON THE GROUND, COP! OR THE BITCH GETS IT IN THE EYE!
ROY!
WHAT, THIS THING? YOU GUYS DON'T NEED TO WORRY ABOUT IT--IT'S MOSTLY FOR SHOW.
TRUTH IS, I ABHOR VIOLENCE.

SEE? THAT'S HOW MUCH I TRUST YOU GUYS.

DAMN RIGHT. NOW--WHERE'S THE TEDDY BEAR?
...TEDDY BEAR? OH, OKAY, SORRY--I DIDN'T REALIZE YOU GUYS WERE HIGH. IT'S OKAY, I CAN WORK WITH THAT--

WE'RE NOT FUCKING AROUND MAN, WHERE IS IT?!

I CAN ASSURE YOU FELLAS, I UNDERSTAND WHAT YOU'RE GOING THROUGH HERE. I HAD ONE WHEN I WAS A KID, GUY MY MOM WAS DATING THREW IT AWAY, SAID I WAS TOO OLD FOR IT.
I STILL FEEL THAT PAIN, EVERY DAY. BUT THAT DOESN'T MEAN IT'S OKAY TO TAKE PEOPLE HOSTAGE.
YOU DO THAT, YOU'RE NO BETTER THAN ISIS!

ISIS! WHAT IS THE MOTHERFUCKER--MAN, JUST GIVE ME THE FUCKING BEAR! I KNOW SHE HID IT WITH YOU! BITCH IS TOO SMART FOR HER OWN--

BLAM

GET 'IM!
BLAMBLAMBLAMBLAMBLAMBLAMBLAM
BLAMBLAMBLAMBLAMBLAMBLAMBLAM
BLAMBLAMBLAMBLAMBLAMBLAMBLAM

FUCK!
FUCK!
FUCK!

TIME TO BE THE BIG GODDAMNED HERO, ROY.

BLINK
BLINK

ALRIGHT...

WHAT THE FUCK WAS THAT?

WE ALL JUST WANT TO BE LOVED.
LOS 5 PINTOS
RE-ELEC
KINCAID
MAYOR
BRUNDO

IT STARTS AT AN EARLY AGE--WHEN WE'RE NOT EVEN SURE WHAT IT IS WE'RE SUPPOSED TO WANT, EXACTLY.
UNDERTAKER

WE SPEND THE NEXT FEW YEARS TRYING TO FIGURE IT OUT AS CLUMSILY AS HUMANLY POSSIBLE.

BY COLLEGE, WE THINK WE'RE GETTING THE HANG OF IT, OF COURSE--
Slipknot

BUT THEN THE TWENTY-FIRST BIRTHDAY HITS AND ALL HELL BREAKS LOOSE.

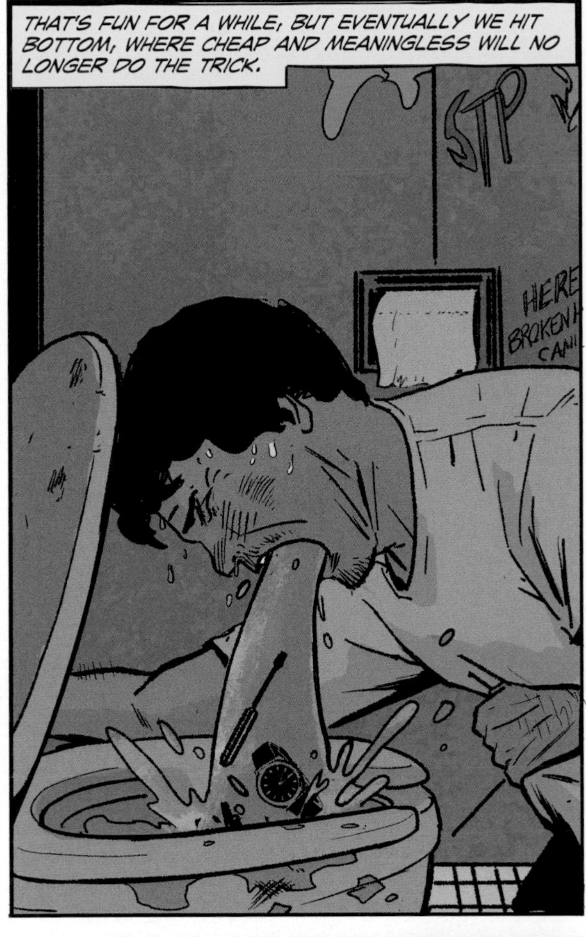
THAT'S FUN FOR A WHILE, BUT EVENTUALLY WE HIT BOTTOM, WHERE CHEAP AND MEANINGLESS WILL NO LONGER DO THE TRICK.

WE START LOOKING FOR SOMETHING DEEPER. A REAL CONNECTION--

THAT'S WHEN YOU SPOT SOMEONE ACROSS A CROWDED ROOM--

AND THE SMILE YOU GET BACK TELLS YOU EVERYTHING YOU NEED TO KNOW.

FROM THERE, IT'S ALL MOMENTUM--
FROM FIRST DATES--

TO ROMANTIC GETAWAYS--

TO NIGHTS ON A COUCH, CURLED UP TOGETHER.

BEFORE WE KNOW IT, WE'RE LOOKING FOR INSANELY OVERPRICED JEWELRY, AND HOPING AND PRAYING TO GOD SHE SAYS--

NO. NO FUCKING WAY, MAC.

EITHER HE GOES--
Rrrrrrrrrrr

OR I GO.
BUT, BABY!
HE'S MY PARTNER!
WHAT HAPPENED TO YOUR OLD PARTNER?
THE ONE WHO LOOKS LIKE HE'S FROM A SEVENTIES PORNO?
ROY? YOU KNOW, I CAN SEE IT, IF YOU ADD A MOUSTACHE. BUT HE'S STILL MY PARTNER, TOO--
AND I TOLD YOU, YOU NEED TO GET RID OF HIM, TOO. HE'S AN ASSHOLE.

AW, SWEETHEART, THAT'S NOT TRUE--
FUME
FUME
YOU JUST HAVEN'T GOTTEN TO KNOW HIM, SWEETHEART. HE IS THE KINDEST, GENTLEST MAN I HAVE EVER KNOWN.

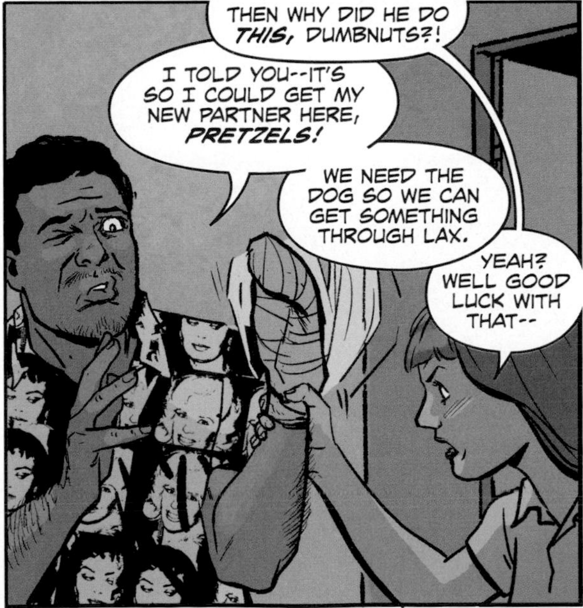
THEN WHY DID HE DO THIS, DUMBNUTS?!
I TOLD YOU--IT'S SO I COULD GET MY NEW PARTNER HERE, PRETZELS!
WE NEED THE DOG SO WE CAN GET SOMETHING THROUGH LAX.
YEAH? WELL GOOD LUCK WITH THAT--

DOG DOESN'T SEEM TO LIKE YOU VERY MUCH.
YEAH, I DON'T GET IT--WHY DID THEY NAME HIM PRETZELS?
HE FUCKING *HATES* PRETZELS!

MAC, *BABY*--
YOU KNOW I DON'T *MEAN* TO BE HARD ON YOU, RIGHT?
YEAH, I KNOW...
IT'S JUST-- *ALL* THE WORK *WE'VE* DONE ON GETTING YOUR FICO SCORE UP, GETTING YOU THAT CROSSFIT MEMBERSHIP...

YOU HAVE SO *MUCH* POTENTIAL, BABY.
AND I HATE TO SEE YOU WASTE IT ON THESE LOSER FRIENDS OF YOURS.
IT MAKES ME FEEL LIKE YOU'RE NOT PUTTING EFFORT INTO *OUR* RELATIONSHIP-- LIKE YOU DON'T CARE.

YOU *DO CARE* ABOUT ME, DON'T YOU, HONEY?
*UH... UH HUH.*

*GOOD.* THEN FIRST THINGS FIRST--GET THIS FUCKING DOG OUT OF MY APARTMENT. HE BARKS, HE GETS FUR ALL OVER EVERYTHING--

AND HE IS SCARING THE *SHIT* OUT OF DUMBLEDORE.
HHHH

BUT BABE, WHERE ARE YOU GOING?!
YOU GOT ME KINDA-- IT WAS A GOOD SPEECH!
LOOK AT YOUR DIRTY PICTURES!

SLAM

AW, NOW I'M JUST GONNA SEE ROY IN ALL OF THESE...

YEAH, LOVE--

FAPFAPFAP
IT'S A COMPLICATED THING.

THE

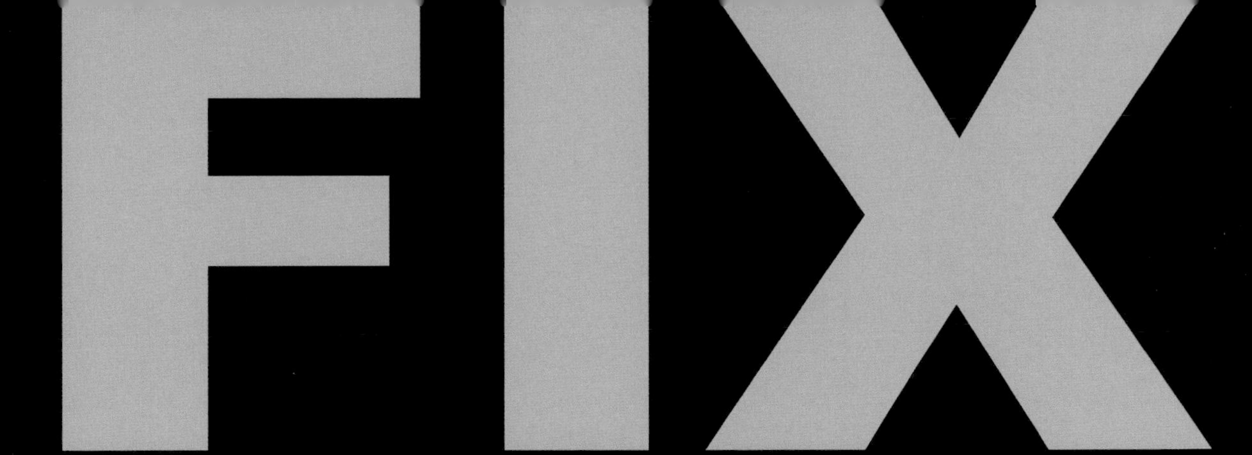
FIX

WHAT?

LAX PARKING

ALL I'M SAYING IS, YOU SHOULD MAYBE TRY TO GROW ONE.
I THINK IT WOULD SUIT YOU.
DING!

HELLO, MAC.

FUCKSTICKS!
OH, I APOLOGIZE. DID WE STARTLE YOU? ARE YOU OKAY? FIND YOUR CENTER--

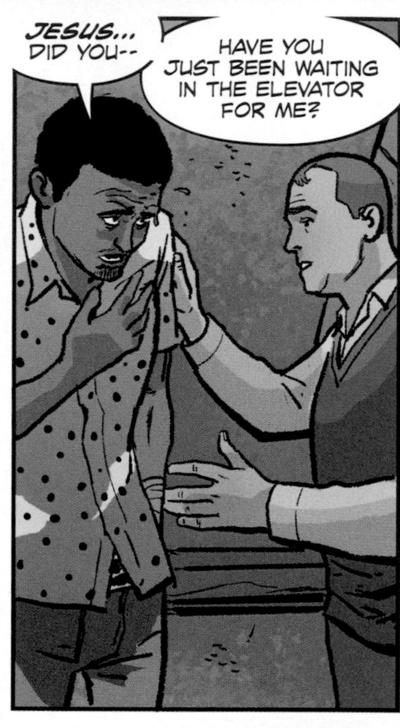
JESUS... DID YOU--
HAVE YOU JUST BEEN WAITING IN THE ELEVATOR FOR ME?

HELLO, MAC.
OH, SORRY.

HELLO, MAC.
OH, SORRY.

HELLO, MAC.
OH, SORRY.

I THOUGHT YOU SAID HE WAS PULLING IN?

...NO.

SO, UH... WHAT ARE YOU DOING HERE, THEN, BOSS?
I MEAN, JOSH...
WHAT DO YOU MEAN? IT'S YOUR FIRST WEEK AT A NEW JOB, MAC. WHAT KIND OF FRIEND WOULD I BE IF I DIDN'T SHOW MY SUPPORT? HERE--
I PACKED YOU A LUNCH.

OH...UH, THANKS...
IT'S NOTHING. SOME QUINOA WITH ORGANIC PEACHES AND HOME-MADE YOGURT.
WHEN YOU SENT OVER YOUR MEAL TRACKER, I WAS DISTURBED BY THE LACK OF FIBER. YOU NEED IT, MAC.

SURE--SURE, I KNOW--
JUST LIKE I NEED CERTAIN THINGS. THAT'S WHY YOU'RE HERE AFTER ALL, RIGHT?
RIGHT.
BUT--I WAS LOOKING AT YOUR DROPCAM FOOTAGE AND--WELL, YOU DON'T SEEM TO BE BONDING WITH, WHAT'S OUR LITTLE FRIEND'S NAME, AGAIN?
PRETZELS.

THE GODDAMN JUNK FOOD LOBBY...

AT ANY RATE, YOU KNOW WE HAVE THREE DOGS OURSELVES, RIGHT? RESCUE PIT BULLS.
THEY GET SUCH A BAD RAP. I LOVE THEM!

HAPPY

BUT THE THING IS, I UNDERSTAND YOUR DILEMMA. FORGING A RELATIONSHIP WITH AN ANIMAL IS A DIFFICULT THING--
I DUNNO WHAT I'M DOING WRONG, BOSS. I'VE TRIED EVERYTHING. TREATS, TOYS--
WELL, YOU KNOW, IT'S THEIR INSTINCTS, MAC. DOGS ARE FANTASTIC JUDGES OF CHARACTER.
EVERY LANDSCAPER MINE HAVE MAULED, WE'VE FOUND THEIR WORK TO BE JUST SUB-PAR.
WHY, THE ONE WHO LOST A HAND, HE WASN'T EVEN USING NATURAL FERTILIZER!

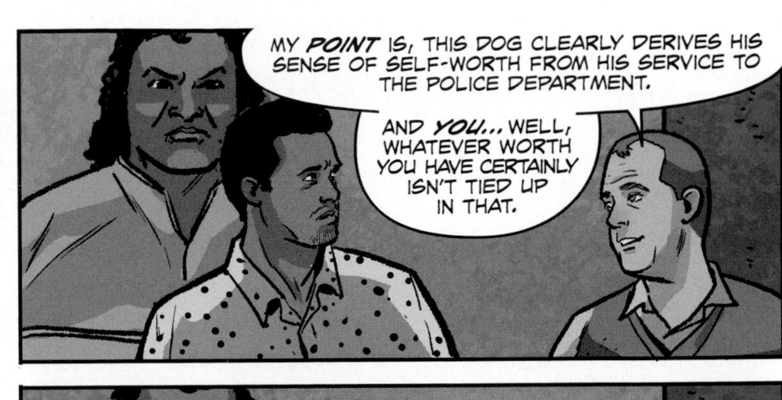
MY POINT IS, THIS DOG CLEARLY DERIVES HIS SENSE OF SELF-WORTH FROM HIS SERVICE TO THE POLICE DEPARTMENT.
AND YOU... WELL, WHATEVER WORTH YOU HAVE CERTAINLY ISN'T TIED UP IN THAT.

I DON'T GET IT--

I'M SAYING THE DOG MAY SENSE YOU WANT TO USE HIM FOR ILLICIT ACTIVITY AND WON'T COOPERATE.

NOW, IF THAT'S THE CASE, WELL--

WE WILL PROUDLY MAKE A LARGE CONTRIBUTION TO A NO-KILL SHELTER IN HIS MEMORY.

YOU OKAY THERE, DETECTIVE?

YOU LOOK LIKE YOU'S A MILLION MILES AWAY!
HUH? OH UH, HEY, SERGEANT.
YEAH, SORRY-- IT'S NOTHING, JUST PERSONAL STUFF.
YOU KNOW HOW IT IS.
LABOUR LAWS

TELL ME ABOUT IT. YOU HEARD ABOUT THIS ANTIBIOTIC RESISTANT GONORRHEA?
WHAT?
POIK
POLICE

SORRY, THOUGHT WE WAS BEING PERSONAL.
YOU READY TO GET OUT ON PATROL?
YEAH, SURE THING-- LET ME JUST GET--
GRRR...

AW, GEEZ. HE'S STILL NOT WARMING UP TO YA, HUH?
NO...
I REALLY DON'T GET IT. I THOUGHT PRETZELS'D BE ALL OVER YOU, YOU BEING THE BIG HERO COP THAT STOPPED THOSE KILLER NUNS AND ALL.
YEAH, WELL, HE DON'T SEEM TOO IMPRESSED. I'M BEIN' NICE TO HIM AS I CAN BE--

WELL, MAYBE THAT'S JUST THE THING. MY OLDEST, HE GOT HIMSELF ONE OF THEM GERBILS? CUTE LITTLE THING, BUT--NASTY. KEPT BITING HIS HAND EVERY TIME HE'D PUT IT IN THE CAGE.
SO'S I TOLD HIM, DEXTER, YOU WANT THE GERBIL TO STOP BITING YOU, YOU'RE GONNA HAVE TO BITE HIM RIGHT BACK!

SO WHAT HAPPENED?
WHAT DO YOU THINK? HE BIT HIM RIGHT BACK!
ROO ROO ROO

AND IT WORKED?
I DUNNO, DAMN THING GOT LOST IN THE HOUSE, WE NEVER SAW IT AGAIN.
ROOTLE ROOTLE

BUT MY POINT IS, MAYBE YOU SHOULD STOP GETTING HIM TO TRY TO LIKE YOU, AND TRY TO GET HIM TO RESPECT YOU.
YEAH?

YEAH! SHOW HIM HOW A REAL LAPD ROBBERY HOMICIDE DETECTIVE CRACKS SOME HEADS--
SMAK!

MAYBE YOU'RE RIGHT.
YOU BET I AM! NOW COME ON--I BET THERE'S ALL KINDS OF REAL SHITSTAINS IN CUSTOMS RIGHT NOW.
Anbeso

YEAH...ALL KINDS...

OH, THAT REMINDS ME--I HAVE AN ASSOCIATE DOING A RUN-THROUGH AT THE AIRPORT TODAY--HE MAY DROP BY AND SAY HELLO.
OKAY--WAIT, THE GOOD HELLO OR THE BAD HELLO?

MAC, COME ON--YOU'RE A VALUABLE MEMBER OF THIS TEAM.

THAT SAID--IF YOU DO RUN INTO HIM, ABOVE ALL, BE FRIENDLY--

"--AND BE POLITE."
SKY MALL
BLANKET
FLY

--SORRY, MISS--
WOULD IT BE POSSIBLE TO GET A RED WINE AS WELL, PLEASE?
YES, OF COURSE, SIR.

PACHONK

PLACE

EXCUSE ME, SORRY--
HRR?
APOLOGIES--IT'S JUST--WOULD YOU MIND TERRIBLY PUTTING YOUR SEAT BACK FOR A BIT?
I WOULD, ACTUALLY.

OF COURSE, IT'S JUST--MY MEAL HAS JUST ARRIVED, YOU SEE--
HUH? NOBODY ELSE'S DID.
THAT'S BECAUSE I ORDERED A SPECIAL MEAL.

WELL, AREN'T YOU SPECIAL.

I UNDERSTAND. IT'S A LONG FLIGHT, ISN'T IT? AND WE'D ALL JUST LIKE TO BE COMFORTABLE, WOULDN'T WE? IT'S THE HUMAN CONDITION.
YEAH, WELL, YOU WANTED TO BE THAT COMFORTABLE, YOU SHOULDA FLOWN FIRST-CLASS.

HA! SO WASTEFUL, THOUGH, ISN'T IT? FIRST-CLASS. I TRY TO KEEP MY EYES SET ON WHAT I NEED, AND ASK FOR NOTHING MORE. THIS SEAT SHOULD MORE THAN SUFFICE, AND IT WAS QUITE THE BARGAIN ON KAYAK.

BUT THEN, THAT'S ANOTHER ASPECT OF THE HUMAN CONDITION, ISN'T IT? LOOKING UPWARD, WANTING, SOMETHING BETTER NO MATTER HOW GOOD WHAT'S ALREADY IN FRONT OF US IS. LIKE YOU, FOR INSTANCE--

YOU HAVE A SEAT, A TRAY, A FANCY LITTLE SCREEN TO WATCH MOVIES ON, THE REST. BUT YOUR EYES ARE HEAVY. YOUR BACK ACHES. SO YOU CONSPIRE TO TAKE ANOTHER MAN'S SPACE, ANOTHER MAN'S COMFORT, TO ASSIST YOUR OWN.
AIRBUS

LOOK, BUDDY--THE SEAT'S GOT A BUTTON THAT MAKES IT GO UP AND DOWN. THAT'S WHAT IT'S THERE FOR. IF YOU GOT A PROBLEM, TAKE IT UP WITH THE FLIGHT ATTENDANT.
OH NO, NO--THERE'S NO NEED FOR THAT. THIS IS A CONTENTIOUS DEBATE IN AIR TRAVEL, I KNOW.

I SAW A STORY ABOUT TWO GENTLEMEN HAVING THIS VERY ARGUMENT, AND THINGS GOT SO HEATED THEY ACTUALLY DIVERTED THE PLANE! CAN YOU IMAGINE?

AND AS MUCH SYMPATHY AS I HAD FOR THE AGGRIEVED--IN MY ESTIMATION--I REALLY WONDERED HOW HE COULD'VE BEEN SO FOOLISH.
AFTER ALL, ALL HE REALLY NEEDED TO DO WAS TAKE NOTE OF THE ADDRESS ON THE LUGGAGE TAG OF THE OFFENDING PARTY'S CARRY-ON.
LIKE YOURS, FOR INSTANCE.
WHITAKER LANE. SOUNDS LOVELY.

THEN, HE COULD'VE SHOWN UP AT THAT MAN'S HOME--LATE WOULD BE BETTER, FOR OBVIOUS REASONS--AND GATHER THE MAN'S WIFE, HIS CHILDREN, HIS HOUSEPETS, INTO THEIR KITCHEN.

THEN, HE COULD'VE CHAINED THE MAN UP AGAINST HIS KITCHEN COUNTER--IT'LL SOUND LIKE A BIT OF STRANGE ANGLE, BUT AT A POINT WHERE THE BOTTOM OF THE MAN'S RIB CAGE JUST MEETS THE TOP OF THE COUNTER.

AND *THEN,* IN FRONT OF *ALL* OF HIS LOVED ONES, HE SHOULD'VE GRABBED THE MAN'S SHOULDERS-- LIKE THIS--AND PULLED BACK, *SLOWLY* BUT *FIRMLY*--

UNTIL THE MAN'S SPINE *SNAPPED,* LEAVING HIM IN A SORT OF PERMANENT RECLINING POSITION.

*YES,* THAT WOULD'VE BEEN A *MUCH* MORE EFFECTIVE RESPONSE, I THINK.

PACHUNK

RED WINE SIR?
*AH,* LOVELY--

CHEERS.

THE THING ABOUT LOVE IS IT COMES IN ALL SHAPES AND SIZES.
IT DOESN'T HAVE TO BE ROMANTIC LOVE, OR BE ABOUT PHYSICAL ATTRACTIVE--
SOMETIMES ALL YOU WANT IS A PARTNERSHIP.
United States
Customs and

MAC BRUNDO HAS HAD PARTNERS--

HE'S MAYBE EVEN BEEN IN LOVE.

BUT THERE WAS ALWAYS SOMETHING MISSING.

SOMETHING WRONG.

BUT THEN MAYBE ALL THOSE NOT-QUITE CONNECTIONS WERE NECESSARY--
SNIFF
SNIFFF

MAYBE THEY HELPED HIM TO BE READY--
FIDDLE
FIDDLE

WHEN HE MET THE **TRUE LOVE** OF HIS LIFE.

LIKE I SAID, LOVE--

BARK
BETTER HOLD ON TIGHT!
IT'S A COMPLICATED THING.

BARK
BARK

CAVIAR &
CAVIAR&CHAMPAGNE
BARK BARK BARK BARK
BARK BARK

BARK
BARK

BA
BAR
BA
B

BARK
BARKBARK
BARK

RRRRPP

RRRRRRR
RRRRRR
FARMERS
RKET
& Fairfax

BARK
BARK
BARK

FREEZE, DON'T MOVE!
CHOMP

GAAAAAAAAAAAAAH
GET HIM OFF ME, GET HIM OFF ME!
TELL US WHERE THE DRUGS ARE!
MY NUTS! MY FUCKING NUTS--

HE'S NOT GONNA LET GO TIL YOU TELL US WHERE THE STASH IS!
I JUST TOLD YOU-- MY NUTS!
g Forclosed
roperties
SSHOLES
DR. MASON ARBOGHAST
LIVE IN LO

I--I GOT TESTICULAR LAST YEAR, AND THEY TOOK ONE OF 'EM--BUT INSTEAD OF THE IMPLANT, I BEEN USING IT, TO SMUGGLE DRUGS TO PAY FOR MY HEALTH CARE BILLS--
WOW, THAT IS...
SCRITCH

SMAK
THAT IS FUCKIN' AWESOME!

MAN, ROY IS GONNA BE SO JEALOUS! IN HIS NUTS?!
THAT IS DEFINITELY GONNA MAKE THE NEWS!

AND JUST LIKE THAT, MAC HAD FOUND SOMETHING.
SOMETHING TRULY SPECIAL--
RIVER TOURS
MIKE WATT VISIT SAN PEDRO
Welcome to LOS ANGELES
KINCAID

LOVELY DOGS, BEAGLES.
YOU'RE TELLIN' ME!
Fruit Stripe
5 JUICY FLAVORS
SOMETHING OTHER PEOPLE YEARN FOR.

YES SIR--A REAL PARTNERSHIP.
ROO ROO ROO

YES, I'VE JUST LANDED. NO, NO, ALL WENT FINE. LET THE CLIENT KNOW--
LODI
BUT THEN, THERE ARE ALL KINDS OF PARTNERSHIPS IN THIS WORLD. SOME GOOD--

SOME...NOT SO GOOD.
--ALL IS IN GOOD HANDS.

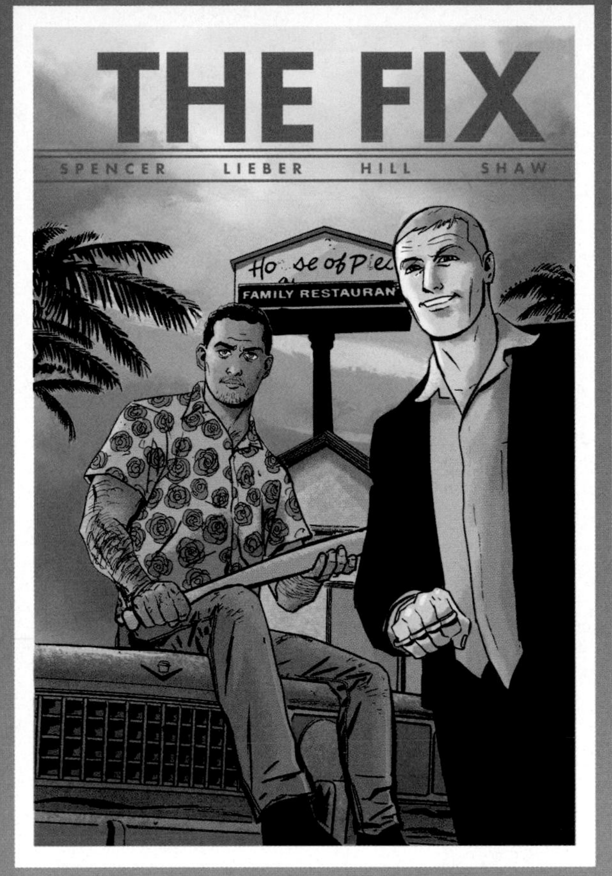
THE FIX
SPENCER LIEBER HILL SHAW
FAMILY RESTAURANT

NICK SPENCER
RYAN HILL
STEVE LIEBER
NIC J SHAW
image
1
006
2
THE
one
image expo
variant
FIX

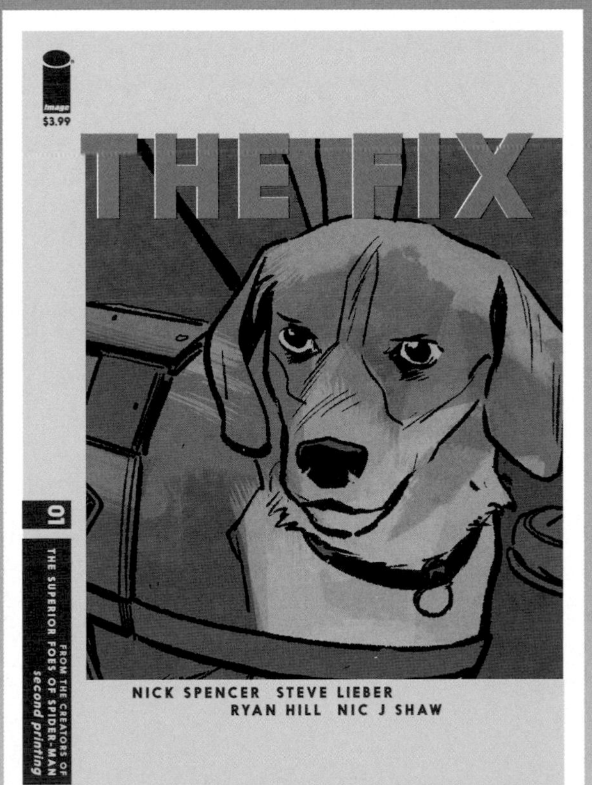
image
$3.99
THE FIX
01
FROM THE CREATORS OF
THE SUPERIOR FOES OF SPIDER-MAN
second printing
NICK SPENCER STEVE LIEBER
RYAN HILL NIC J SHAW

ISSUE 01 // THIRD PRINTING
NICK SPENCER // STEVE LIEBER
RYAN HILL // NIC J SHAW
THE
FIX
image
#1
3.99

*Issue Two*
*Second Printing*
*Third Printing*

*Issue Three*
*Regular Cover*

## THE FIX

COVER GALLERY

Issue One
Regular Cover
Image Expo Variant
Second Printing
Third Printing
Fourth Printing
Fifth Printing

Issue Two
Regular Cover

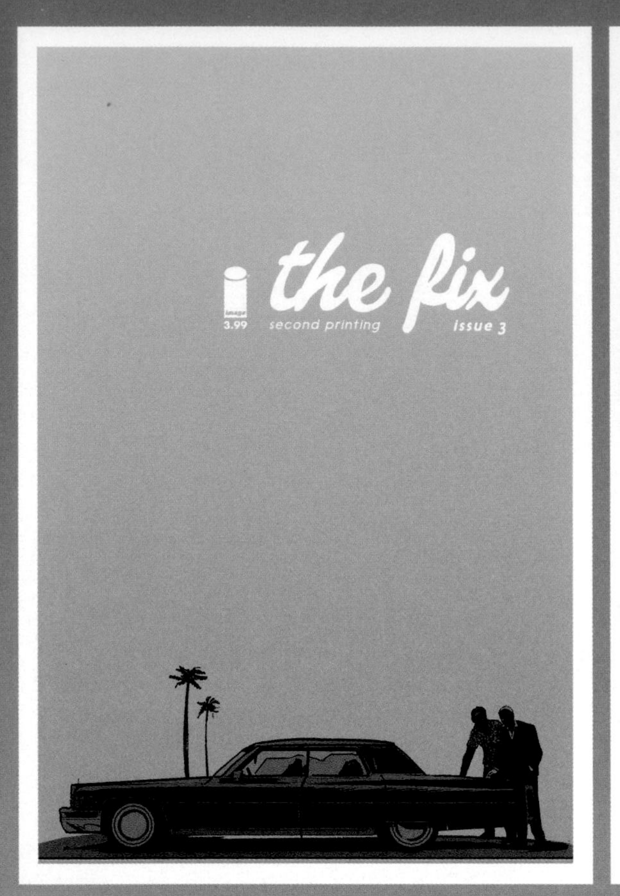

*Issue Three*
*Second Printing*

*Issue Four*
*Regular Cover*
*Second Printing*